Hugh McLeave was born and educated in the west of Scotland, and served as an artillery officer during the Second World War. A highly-acclaimed and prolific author, he has had twenty-five books published, both fiction and non-fiction. He currently lives in France.

THE BONAPARTE PLOT

In 1803 it seems nothing can stop Napoleon Bonaparte from invading and conquering England. So Prime Minister William Pitt plans to thwart his enemy. He recruits French royalist General Georges Cadoudal, with orders to kidnap or kill Bonaparte and restore the Bourbon monarchy . . . But Bonaparte, a master tactician, detects and unravels the murder plot. In order to rule as Emperor of France, he constructs a plan that will cost many lives . . . This fictional account is based on the testimony of Bonaparte himself and his contemporaries.

HUGH McLEAVE

THE BONAPARTE PLOT

Complete and Unabridged

ULVERSCROFT
Leicester

First published in Great Britain in 2005 by
Robert Hale Limited
London

First Large Print Edition
published 2006
by arrangement with
Robert Hale Limited
London

British Library CIP Data

McLeave, Hugh
The Bonaparte plot.—Large print ed.—
Ulverscroft large print series: adventure & suspense
1. Napoleon, I, Emperor of the French, 1769 – 1821
—Assassination attempts—Fiction
2. Cadoudal, Georges, 1771 – 1804 —Fiction
3. France—History—Consulate and First Empire,
1799 – 1815 —Fiction 4. Historical fiction
5. Large type books
I. Title
823.9'14 [F]

ISBN 1–84617–441–4

Published by
F. A. Thorpe (Publishing)
Anstey, Leicestershire

Set by Words & Graphics Ltd.
Anstey, Leicestershire
Printed and bound in Great Britain by
T. J. International Ltd., Padstow, Cornwall

This book is printed on acid-free paper

BOOK I

'What a novel, my life!'

Napoleon to Count Emmanuel de las Cases on Saint Helena

1

When Joséphine came into her yellow salon expecting to find him dressed, she discovered he had fallen asleep on a sofa; firelight flickered across his wan, exhausted face framed in lank, dark hair and fell on the snuff marks on his white waistcoat and the inkstains on his white buckskin breeches where he would often wipe his quill pen. Bending over him, she grasped his right hand and squeezed; his blue-grey eyes fluttered open and focused on her face.

'Bonaparte, we'll be late if you don't hurry.'

'Late for what?'

'You remember, the opera.'

Now, he recalled promising to take Joséphine and his step-daughter, Hortense, to the first Paris performance of Joseph Haydn's 'Creation'. Only, he felt more like having dinner in front of this fire and going to bed. 'You go on without me,' he grumbled. 'I'll stay here.'

'But all the papers have announced you'll be there,' she protested. 'Think of all the people waiting to see you, and how disappointed they'll be.'

3

'Hmm. Last time I went to the opera four months ago, that Italian sculptor, Ceracchi, and his gang were waiting to knife me. Anyway, I don't give a damn about Austrian church music.'

'Garat is singing,' she insisted. He shrugged his indifference, reaching out a booted foot to kick the fire into life.

'All right then, it's Christmas Eve,' Joséphine cried. 'Surely you can give yourself one night off.' She ran a fragile, fine-boned hand over his face then kissed him. 'For me,' she whispered.

At that he nodded, hoisted himself to his feet and barked an order which brought his staff officer, General Jean Rapp, his secretary, Bourrienne, and his valet, Constant, into the salon. Within minutes, Constant had dressed him in silk shirt, silk stockings and buckled shoes, cashmere waistcoat and new buckskin breeches; over this, he drew on his green horse-guards jacket with its scarlet piping and braided rank badges of a colonel.

When he came downstairs, Joséphine and Hortense were waiting in the main Tuileries salon; he kissed his stepdaughter, glanced appraisingly at his wife then frowned. 'It's freezing fog outside,' he snapped. 'You'll catch your death in that nightdress.' With his unsheathed sword he lifted the train of the filmy muslin gown which revealed more than it hid and pursed his lips at the flimsy satin slippers underneath. 'Put something over your shoulders,' he said.

'Claire, go and fetch my shawl,' Joséphine said to her companion, Madame de Rémusat, knowing Bonaparte's modesty. When she returned with the Paisley shawl, he grimaced. English muslin and a Scottish shawl while he was fighting for his survival against Pitt and his European allies! Yet, how could he complain? His own troops had brought back the fashion for shawls from the Egyptian campaign.

'Rapp will show me how Egyptian women wear them,' Joséphine said, smiling.

Bonaparte knew his wife too well to kick his heels waiting for her performance. Jamming his bicorn hat on his head, he called for his carriage. 'Don't keep the opera house waiting too long,' he muttered, as he marched with his brisk, jerky stride to the door followed by two of his generals, the cavalry guard commander Jean-Baptiste Bessieres and his aide, the Marquis de Lauriston. Outside, in the snow-covered court of the Tuileries Palace, General Jean Lannes stood with his consular horse guards deployed round the two berlin coaches which would take the First Consul and his party to the opera. Lannes took his place with the other two generals beside Bonaparte.

'I see we have that drunken coachman César, again,' the First Consul barked.

'He was with you in Italy and at the battle of the Pyramids, General,' Lannes said, well aware that this excused everything with Bonaparte.

'Get a move on, man,' Bonaparte shouted, and the driver hiccupped at the horses.

They trotted past the stables and between the guards' pavilions. Before the coach had reached the end of the Rue de Rivoli, which they were constructing, Bonaparte had retracted his chin into his coat collar, pulled his hat over his eyes and fallen asleep with the bells of Saint-Roch church ringing in his ears. Even in battle, he had this facility for blocking out his consciousness as though snuffing a candle.

However, tonight vivid images still flitted through his sleep. Later he would wonder if his inner mind had associated the present danger with the previous attempt on his life at the opera house, and with his narrow escape when crossing the flooded Tagliamento River during his first Italian campaign in 1797. As he dozed in the jogging coach, his mind backtracked and he was fording the icy waters in a carriage that threatened to sink or shatter under Austrian cannon fire from the direction of the snow-covered Carinthian Mountains beyond the other bank of the river; it was midnight, and they had nothing to follow but the torches held aloft by General Murat's cavalry. At any moment, he felt a slip would end his life in the freezing Tagliamento. Each detail of that nightmare ride returned — the water swirling through the coach and spouting from the impact of cannonballs, the crash of muskets, the screams of the wounded, the feeling it was his last moment.

Now his carriage with its horse guards was leaving the Tuileries. Nobody spotted a shadowy figure signal to someone further on as they turned left into Rue Saint-Nicaise, a cobbled passage ending in Rue de la Loi which then ran nearly a kilometre to the opera house. 'Vive Bonaparte . . . Vive le Petit Caporal,' came the shouts of passers-by celebrating Christmas for the first time since its cancellation by the Revolutionary Council seven years before. Inside the coach, the three generals heard the driver curse as he swerved at the last minute to avoid a horse and cart almost straddling the murky street; his horses tripped over a pile of rocks and the berlin bucked and swayed as it rumbled over them.

No sooner had they passed the obstacle than the whole universe seemed to erupt around them. A blinding flash and detonation pierced Bonaparte's reverie and the blast which followed hurled the heavy coach, its horses, driver, occupants and two attendants high into the air. Miraculously, the vehicle and the animals dropped plumb and the horses managed to stagger forward.

'We've been blown up,' Bonaparte shouted. Now fully awake and alert, he heard the whine of metal ricocheting off the buildings, the rumble of falling masonry and the screams of guardsmen and their horses cut to pieces by the detonation and the iron shot.

'Stop the coach!' General Lannes yelled.

Bonaparte shut him up. 'Drive on!' he bellowed.

'But Madame Bonaparte . . . ' Lannes said.

'She's too far behind,' Bonaparte snapped. 'Get going, man,' he shouted to the driver and the fuddled man whipped the two white horses onward, into the Rue de la Loi where the street lanterns between the houses were still see-sawing with the impact of the explosion. Pedestrians and revellers scattered before the terrified horses which galloped full-out all the way to the opera.

Of the four generals who walked into the foyer of the opera and took their places in the box reserved for the First Consul, only Bonaparte looked calm and unruffled. All chatter ceased and everyone froze. Then from the orchestra stalls through the gilt and glitter of the tiered boxes to the 'gods' beneath the roof, the whole audience rose to its feet to cheer him.

Like the powder train that had fired the explosive in the Rue Saint-Nicaise, word of the murder attempt had run round the opera house; anyway, all Paris had heard the blast and those late-comers had observed the consular coach standing outside with its windows shattered and its white horses bloodstained. For fully five minutes everyone applauded the young general who had done more than any other to restore order and bring glory to France. Men sighed and women wept with relief, thinking of what might have happened to the country had he been assassinated.

Before the applause died down a new burst of cheering greeted Joséphine's arrival. Bonaparte noticed Hortense was bleeding from a cut on her arm and was sobbing with fright, like her mother. 'You're all right, aren't you?' he asked his wife, while Lauriston went to find a bandage.

'Yes, but I thought they had killed you,' she sobbed.

'They nearly murdered us both,' he muttered, reflecting once again that his lucky star had saved him as it had done on so many battlefields: a drunken driver who went faster than the assassins had estimated; a gauzy Paisley shawl that had taken a minute or two longer to tie. These trivial things had foiled the murder plot.

Still shocked by the nightmare experience of driving over the dead and dying and surviving herself by a second or two, Joséphine whispered her account of the drama to Bonaparte; she had fainted when the gunpowder had detonated in front of them, but Rapp had turned the coach round among the victims and taken another route.

'*Scélérats*,' Bonaparte muttered. 'Monsters who will kill so many innocent people because they hate me.' He gave the signal for the orchestra and chorus to begin their performance of Haydn's 'Creation' and the opera house settled down.

Lannes and the other two generals had disappeared to supervise the rescue operations, so Bonaparte moved back into the shadows of the box. When Joséphine looked round he seemed to be fast asleep, but she did not disturb him, aware he never liked church music or even court music; he preferred 'La Marseillaise' or 'Ça Ira' or military marches played at almost double their tempo to keep his troops striding along

10

quickly enough to throw the enemy off-balance and help him win his battles. Ten minutes later, when she glanced backwards, she noticed he had slipped away.

On his way back to the Tuileries, Bonaparte stopped to inspect the carnage in Rue Saint-Nicaise. By the light of guttering torches, candles and oil lanterns, he saw bodies and fragments of flesh and bone piled high where the casualty squads from l'Hotel-Dieu and other hospitals had dumped them; carts and cabriolets were transporting the injured to hospitals and army surgeons were giving first-aid to some of the wounded. Bonaparte stopped to say a word of encouragement to the most gore-stained of his consular guard. He walked round several dead horses lying on the cobbled street and watched soldiers collect the grisly debris of others, literally wrenched apart by the blast. Not a window or a door in the short street remained undamaged and several tall buildings had lost their façades and roofs.

From a gaping hole where revellers had been celebrating Christmas in the Café d'Apollon, stretcher-bearers were emerging with the dead and injured. General Lannes whispered that at least ten people had died and twenty-eight were injured; they were evacuating fifty houses which would collapse.

Lannes reckoned they had all escaped by a matter of five seconds.

'Any of the people in the street see anything, Lannes?'

'There was a horse and cart near the Rue Saint-Honoré . . . some people say there was a girl holding it.'

Bonaparte deliberated for a moment. Every one of those horses ridden by his dragoon guard would bear an army brand and the mark and number of the farrier who had shod them. 'Sift every piece of horseflesh in the street and find me what's left of the horse the child was holding,' he ordered. 'Get the farrier sergeant at the barracks to help identify all our own horses.'

'I have already put that in hand, General.'

'Good thinking, Lannes.' Bonaparte wondered if he had misjudged this general whose reckless courage always seemed in inverse proportion to his intellect.

'It was Fouché who told us to pick up every bit of evidence and take it to the police ministry. He has just left.'

'Fouché?' Bonaparte repeated. His minister of police had lost no time. Did that scoundrel have advance notice of the plot? He seemed to have an uncanny and ghoulish flair for materializing on the scene of the crime.

Back in the Tuileries, he ran upstairs

towards his own study. Outside, two men were sitting, talking in whispers. His foreign minister, Charles-Maurice de Talleyrand-Périgord, and his police minister, Joseph Fouché. When he had given himself a few minutes to reflect and work up his rage, the First Consul sent Rapp to summon Fouché who glided across the parquet floor without seeming to touch it or leave any incriminating trace. Before he had twitched his head forward in obeisance, Bonaparte let fly with the full fury of his Corsican temper.

'Well, your friends nearly had me tonight, Fouché. What went wrong with their murder plot?'

'My friends, Consul?'

'Your Jacobin friends who thought up these gunpowder plots in the first place,' Bonaparte yelled. Ten weeks before, Fouché had arrested a group of diehard republican extremists (Jacobins) who had blueprinted an assassination attempt like the present one; they had planned to stop the First Consul's coach with wire snares then fling a bomb full of gunpowder and shrapnel at him. 'Since you are a past-president of the Jacobin Club why didn't you foresee the plot and arrest the other murderers?'

'Because, sire, I believe the plotters were royalists,' Fouché murmured.

Bonaparte went to ram his right boot into the coal fire, stirring it into a blaze as though to symbolize his own wrath; he fixed Fouché with those blue-grey eyes that appeared to change colour with his moods. 'Maybe you want to get rid of me in the way you got rid of your friend Robespierre. You're a traitor, Fouché, a traitor to the marrow.' He began pacing up and down his study with that peculiar marionette walk and intriguing twitch of his right shoulder. 'How many people have you had butchered with cannon or the guillotine — apart from Robespierre and Louis XVI? Perhaps I should have your head before you have mine.'

'There I must disagree with you, sire,' Fouché murmured, his voice completely neutral.

Bonaparte gazed at the balefully ugly and bloodless spectre. Nobody ever knew what this man thought, how many state or private secrets lay behind that fish-eyed, alabaster look. Bonaparte knew Fouché even had him, the First Consul, under surveillance wherever he went.

He couldn't go to the lavatory without a report about it appearing on this man's desk; he bribed the spendthrift Joséphine to worm palace secrets out of her — yes, even the details of his sexual prowess; he doubled

14

the sums that he, Bonaparte, paid his mistresses to record his pillow-talk; he had Bourrienne, his secretary, under his thumb and God-knew-how many of his staff; he traded royalist emigrants off against republicans and the other way round; he had a web of political spies covering Europe from Dublin to the Danube and a skein of informants throughout France which included counts and courtesans, politicians and common prostitutes.

Yet, Fouché had his uses; he had backed him during those dangerous days of the *coup d'état* in October 1799 when he had overthrown the five-man Directory, which had succeeded the revolutionary governments; he had helped to make him First Consul. Who among his henchmen had briefed him about the state of the country better than Fouché, the master spy?

For his part, Fouché was scrutinizing his master under hooded eyelids. He knew the signs of genuine anger and he understood Bonaparte's Italian streak of *commedia dell'arte*; anger meant opaque eyes, the voice pitched half an octave higher and the ringing, singing Corsican accent. Bonaparte was prepared to listen tonight.

'So Fouché, it's not your Jacobin friends who tried to kill me tonight.'

'It was a royalist plot prepared by the Chouans.'

Bonaparte sneered. 'You're covering up for your republican friends. That effete royalist bunch would never dare try anything.'

'They have some determined men.'

'What would they gain?'

'They see you as the ruler of France, so they think if they get rid of you they can restore the monarchy.'

'But they know I have told the man who calls himself Louis XVIII he would have to walk over a hundred thousand dead Frenchmen to recover the Bourbon throne.'

'Well, they think they can reduce that to one dead body — yours.'

'How many times have your Jacobin friends tried to kill me?'

'Five times, sire.'

'All right, so you'll have to prove to me that the infernal machine in Rue Saint-Nicaise had a royalist stamp on it.'

'I will,' Fouché said, quietly.

'You have two weeks,' Bonaparte said. 'In the meantime, prepare a list of your old guillotine friends from the Reign of Terror who have voted my death. We can exile them and kill two birds with one stone.' He flicked his wrist in a gesture of dismissal and Fouché took his leave with that backward shuffle as

16

though fearing a knife in the back. Traitors like Fouché trusted no one and nothing, believing everyone else to be like themselves.

For several minutes Bonaparte paced back and forth, alone with his thoughts. Fouché was right; he did count as the man who held the destiny of France in his hands; he could still hear the echo of all those people in the opera house shouting their relief that he had survived. Maybe those very people who were trying to murder him would rue the day when France grew so frightened of losing him it would plead with him to create his own dynasty. An intriguing thought.

At his behest, Talleyrand, his foreign minister, entered with that sliding, shuffling step with which he disguised the limp caused by his deformed right foot. He seemed the antithesis of Fouché with his elegant dress coat, his ruffed cravat and lace cuffs and those bright eyes darting everywhere, though the square face in which they were set did not move an inch. Yet, both his ministers had started their careers in the church, Fouché at a northern seminary and the rich, aristocratic Talleyrand even becoming Bishop of Autun. Bonaparte glared at the inscrutable mask under the powdered wig.

What had Marat said about Talleyrand during the turbulent days of the Revolution?

You could plant a foot in that man's arse without his face betraying the slightest sign. With poisonous characters like Fouché and Talleyrand around, did he need plotters who used gunpowder and the dagger? Still, of all his ministers, they had proved the most effective and useful.

'Well, did you expect to find me alive?'

'Sire, it will take more than a handful of Jacobins to kill someone like you.'

'Oh, so you think they were Jacobins, too?'

'Shall we ever know?'

'I've given Fouché two weeks to bring me the criminals.'

'A man like Fouché should know where to look,' Talleyrand murmured.

'What do you mean?'

'A man always knows where to find something he has hidden himself.'

'Don't talk like an idiot,' Bonaparte cried. 'Fouché doesn't trust his Jacobin friends and he stands to lose his head if I go and the Bourbons return.' He gave a wry grin. 'You, too. If he voted Louis XVI's death, you did nothing to stop them cutting his head off.'

Unperturbed, Talleyrand produced a silver filigree snuffbox and proffered it; Bonaparte took a pinch of snuff then pocketed the box, ignoring his minister's injured look.

'I don't mean, sire, you were meant to die,'

Talleyrand said, 'merely that you were meant to be grateful to the man who discovers the plotters.'

'Hmm. So, you think Fouché arranged the assassination attempt to get credit for finding the criminals.'

'He does seem to know where to look.'

'That's because he's the best policeman in Europe,' Bonaparte rapped out, then jerked a hand to signify the audience had ended.

★ ★ ★

Several days later, General Rapp came to Bonaparte. 'César, the coachman, would like a word with you, General,' he said. Bonaparte, who allowed hardly anyone into his study, marched through to the salon where César was standing, twisting his bicorn hat in his hands. Bonaparte glared at the pock-marked face and bloodshot eyes.

'Well, man, you wanted to see me?'

'*Oui, mon général*. It's like this you see, I was drunk the other night — '

'So drunk you thought they were firing a twenty-one gun salute when they were trying to kill me.'

'I'm sorry, *mon général* . . . '

'Sorry means nothing and is always too late,' he snapped, turning away.

'But wait . . . ' César stuttered. 'My friends gave me a dinner to celebrate last night.'

Bonaparte looked round, smiling. 'To celebrate what?'

'Well, it's like this . . . they thought I saved their general's life.'

'So, what do you want me to do — give you a medal?'

'*Non, mon général*. But at this party one of my cab-driver pals whispered he saw the cart with the barrel of gunpowder coming out of an entrance and he knew who'd done the job.'

'Where man?' Bonaparte barked. 'What entrance?'

'That's it, *mon général*,' César muttered, shaking his head sadly. 'I can't rightly remember where.'

'No matter. Go and find your cab-driver friend and bring him here.'

'Only one thing, *mon général* . . . there were three or four hundred drivers at the party in the Relais du Marais.'

'And you got so drunk you can't remember who the man was.'

'I couldn't help it . . . they forced it on me . . . wine, brandy, rum.' He ran his tongue over cracked lips.

'One of the penalties of being a hero, César,' Bonaparte grunted. 'Now get out of here and round up every coachman in Paris until you find that man. If you fail, hand in your uniform and don't let me see you again. *Compris?*'

When César had gone, Bonaparte ordered his coach and drove to the ministry of police in the Rue des Saints-Pères. Fouché, he noticed, thrust all his dossiers into drawers, out of sight, as soon as he appeared in his office.

'Get hold of every cab-driver in Paris,' he ordered the minister. 'One of them saw the infernal machine.'

'I'm already doing that, Consul,' Fouché said. When he outlined the operation he had mounted, even Bonaparte admitted he had planned none of his campaigns more thoroughly. Fouché had not only summoned every cab-driver and coachman in Paris to his office, but every cart-driver, horse trader, farrier, saddler, wheel-wright and barrel-maker in the capital; Bonaparte listened, marvelling, as his police minister detailed the list of prostitutes, hotel staff, concierges, café-owners and shopkeepers he had interviewed from the Marais district.

'But do you expect all these people to co-operate?' he asked.

'I've yet to meet the man or woman who did not have at least one reason for co-operating,' Fouché murmured, in a way that Bonaparte felt chilled even the cold atmosphere in that room. His police had already run down and questioned almost everyone in the Rue Saint-Nicaise that night, and every relative of every victim.

Then, in his devious manner, Fouché produced his trump card, citing facts that sent an icy frisson through the First Consul. They had learned a girl was holding the black horse in the middle of the street that night and they had recovered fragments of her body. That morning, Fouché had traced her mother who confirmed someone had paid the child several sous to watch the horse and cart near the Café d'Apollon.

Fouché had her name and description; she was Marianne Pausol from Rue du Bac. For a moment, Bonaparte forgot his own danger; his mind pictured that ragged, red-haired urchin of fourteen, bribed with a few coins by someone who knew she would end as a thousand fragments of mangled flesh.

'Put every man you have on to finding out where she was and who saw her that night and you'll trace the murderers,' Bonaparte said.

'Two hundred of my policemen are doing nothing else,' Fouché replied.

A week later, he came to say they had

located the cabman who had spotted the infernal machine emerging from a coach-hirer's in Rue Paradis; there, they discovered traces of gunpowder in a shed and the proprietor had described three men who had assembled, bit by bit, a vast barrel of powder and shrapnel. They had also unearthed the farrier who had identified his own brand on the horseshoes.

Bonaparte stifled his surprise and admiration. 'And they're Jacobins, I suppose,' he snapped.

'No, Consul. Royalists.'

To Bonaparte's amazement, he flourished a list of known royalists, all embroiled in uprisings in Brittany, Normandy and La Vendée from the outset of the Revolution just over ten years before. 'A gang of royalists arrived in Paris at the end of November and I had my detectives follow them,' Fouché said.

'But not closely enough,' Bonaparte grunted.

'They all have too many friends in your capital,' came the barbed retort.

'These three men — who are they?'

'The Marquis de Limoelan, an aristocrat who has stirred up a lot of trouble in La Vendée. The second man's a little rogue called Saint-Réjant, who claims he's a Breton knight. He has made a name in the north-west for holding up and robbing post coaches and their passengers and using the money to arm his Chouan bands. The third's an old naval rating called Jean-François Carbon, known as Little Frank.'

'He's the man to go for.'

'We've already arrested him,' Fouché murmured in that neutral tone. 'He was hiding in a convent in Rue Notre Dame des Champs'

'Threaten him with summary trial and the guillotine,' Bonaparte barked. 'Nothing clears a man's head like the notion of having it chopped off.'

Soon afterwards, Carbon, a simple Breton sailor in his thirties, broke completely and babbled what he knew of the plot: Limoelan and Saint-Réjant had organized everything between them; Saint-Réjant had experimented with fuses and timed the First Consul's route to the opera; Limoelan gave the girl a few sous to hold the horse across the road; Carbon and Limoelan had stood at the corner of the Tuileries to warn Saint-Réjant, but in the darkness and mist he failed to see them and fired the powder barrel too late. Saint-Réjant was now lying, injured, in a lodging-house in Rue Prouvaire.

Fouché's ace policeman, the giant inspector Pierre-Jean Pasques, found Chevalier

Pierre Robinson de Saint-Réjant lying in a room in a slum with several broken ribs; a tiny figure, less than five feet tall with hollow cheeks and a long, turned-up nose, he was one of the most intrepid of Breton Royalists, the wild Chouans. He made no attempt to deny trying to kill Bonaparte, only lamented his failure. Surprised by the speed of the Consul's cavalcade, he had to light a short fuse and the explosion had catapulted him into the air and against a wall, crushing his ribs and all but killing him. He alone had plotted the assassination. Carbon was a yokel who did not realize what he was doing.

Fouché knew the little man was lying. They coaxed and threatened him; they tried bribing him with 50,000 francs and a command in the republican army; they crushed his thumbs and scorched his flesh. He revealed nothing more. They could behead him a hundred times, face upwards, and he would welcome the red, blood-spattered arms of the guillotine since he would be dying for Christ, his king and his cause without betrayal.

Stocks of gunpowder and unburnt fuses in his room, and witnesses who remembered a funny homunculus in ermine-lined jacket, silk waistcoat and russet breeches behind a spavined black nag and a rickety cart on Christmas Eve gave Fouché enough proof to indict him and Carbon.

Also, a scrawled letter dated 29 December, 1800, which read:

> *My dear Soyer* (Saint-Réjant's code-name)
> *I have heard your news from two friends. As for you, you still haven't learned to write. Alas, the fortnight has come and gone; terrible things are happening. If our misfortunes continue I don't know what will become of us all. We rely on you alone. Your friends remember you and place their fate in your hands. Adieu.*
> *Your sincere friend, Gideon.*
> *We watch every post for your news.*

Gideon was another code-name. All the other members of Saint-Réjant's gang had fled to hide in Brittany or in England. Some like the Marquis de Limoelan and a young man called Coster-Saint-Victor had sailed to America.

For a year, Saint-Réjant and Carbon lay in Bicêtre Prison before being brought to trial in April 1801; both went to the guillotine, shrouded in red hoods, which did not prevent Saint-Réjant from proclaiming, loud and clear, his defiance of Bonaparte and his loyalty to the Bourbons from the scaffold.

Fouché emerged with all the credit, having proved his point that Chouan royalists had planned the murder attempt. But he did not tell Bonaparte everything. In such dubious times when the country changed hands every few years, a man had to watch his back and keep his own counsel. How many leaders had he survived since the Revolution? Who could say when a bomb or a knife thrust might not end Bonaparte's rule?

Fouché therefore kept a few things to himself. Like the fact that the Gideon who had signed that cryptic letter to Saint-Réjant was none other than Georges Cadoudal, most uncompromising of all royalist generals, who could muster and arm more than 20,000 Chouans in Brittany and La Vendée.

And behind Cadoudal stood the exiled Bourbon princes, the two brothers of the executed Louis XVI and their aristocratic contingent. Especially the Count of Artois, who had sought refuge in England where he was scheming a return of the monarchy.

Already, Fouché had a dozen agents in London. But he needed someone who could penetrate the Artois circles, someone to act as a listening-post or even an *agent-provocateur*. Someone with blue-blood friends and no moral qualms about spying on them. Now, what was the name of that wretch who was lying in the fortress prison on the island of Oléron, off the Brittany coast?

Soon, Fouché was looking at the man's police file. Jean-Claude Hippolyte Mehée de la Touche, prodigal son of a famous Parisian surgeon. His record revealed he had spied in Poland, Russia and England for Louis XVI's government but had turned his coat so many times he no longer understood where his loyalties lay. He had sold passports to émigré nobles then betrayed them to the republicans; he had trafficked in everything from liquor to arms; to more countries than he could remember he had hawked secrets and plots hatched only in his own drunken and disordered brain. Yet, he had a royalist background and connections in the Artois retinue. Why not let him peep at the guillotine then buy his release by making a visit to England to find out what the royalists were really plotting?

For Fouché told no one of his other conviction — that the Saint-Réjant plot had an English birthmark. Not only through Artois, but also through the British Government.

France's inveterate enemy had already poured scores of millions of pounds into paying and arming rebel forces in Brittany and Normandy to overthrow the republican government. And, behind every move made by the Chouan rebels and the exiled royalists lay the sinister hand of France's and Bonaparte's most implacable enemy: the British statesman, William Pitt.

2

Every now and again across the back gardens of Downing Street, strident commands and a ragged clatter of muskets and undisciplined feet filtered to the four men seated around the massive mahogany table in the office of the First Lord of the Treasury, reminding them of the crisis facing England. Two thousand volunteers had mustered for evening drill in St James's Park, fifty times that number had reported for duty throughout London and a million more recruits were standing to elsewhere in the country. No one talked or thought of anything but the hour that Bonaparte would throw his armies across the Channel.

They had dined well, the four men in Number Ten Downing Street. Waiters cleared away the trolleys of cold meats, roast beef, venison, pheasant, cheeses and pudding then replenished the port. Since dinner, the quartet had emptied three decanters of full-bodied port and a fourth was circulating as King George III's First Minister, Henry Addington, spoke.

'We have naval intelligence, confirmed by

our French agents, that Bonaparte is in Boulogne to inspect his armies and the fleet that will transport them,' he said.

'Ay, but he has as much chance of getting his barges over the Channel as those troop-carrying balloons his crack-headed inventor has built,' a long-faced man retorted, in a burring, lilting Scots accent. Henry Dundas, newly created Lord Melville, had served as Navy Treasurer for more than a decade and then as War Secretary in Pitt's government. 'Bonaparte's admirals are well aware they have to get by Cornwallis and Nelson — and that means no invasion.'

'All he needs are three days of fog to give him passage across the Channel,' Addington replied. 'And we all know his luck.'

'And his genius.'

As he spoke, William Pitt poured himself half a pint of port and took a long pull. 'While other generals are fighting by the old text books, he's writing new ones. Who'd have wagered a dud penny he'd drive an army with several hundred cannon across the High Alps then thrash the Austrians at Marengo? Who'd have given him the chance of reaching, let alone occupying, Egypt?'

Pitt put down the ornate port-wine glass with its thistle motif. 'No, gentlemen, Bonaparte has calculated his chances of landing his army across the Channel, and with the weather on his side, he could do what the Normans did seven hundred and fifty years ago.'

'We have more than a million men under arms,' Addington objected.

'And we haven't fought a battle here since beating Bonnie Prince Charlie's poorly armed Highlanders at Culloden more than half a century ago,' Pitt snapped. 'I'd give us a week before the French took London.'

Pitt had come to look on Bonaparte almost as a personal enemy as well as the symbol of France's bid for world conquest. For eight of his fifteen years in office he, with his friend and drinking companion, Dundas, had masterminded the war against France.

But just when they were beginning to gain the upper hand, Bonaparte appeared on the scene to change the course of the war with his military and political genius coupled with tactics and strategy no one had ever witnessed before. Pitt had watched two of his coalitions of European powers crumple before the fury of French armies and, more than any one, he knew that only brilliant admirals like Nelson, Howe and Cornwallis had saved England from the fate of Austria, Prussia, Italy, Holland, Belgium and lesser countries. He had poured British gold into the Continent to finance armies; he had used the navy, arms, money to back the many insurrections of Chouan royalists in Brittany, La Vendée and Normandy. Yet no one, it seemed, could stand against General Napoleon Bonaparte, First Consul of France.

Pitt had just spent two years out of office as Warden of the Cinque Ports. He had personally drilled volunteers in his residence at Walmer Castle and realized only too well that Bonaparte would scatter these raw militiamen like chaff if ever he ferried his crack divisions across the Channel. He recalled how everyone thought Bonaparte had fought himself and France to a standstill only to see him cross the Alps, crush the Austrians and grab their European possessions along the Rhine. Not long afterwards, Pitt had resigned office, ostensibly over Catholic emancipation; but truly to restore his broken health and spirits.

His friend Addington had formed a government to sign the Peace of Amiens with France in March 1802, although everyone realized this marked nothing more than stalemate in the long conflict. A year later, the quarrel ignited again over French occupation of the Low Countries, which Bonaparte refused to surrender, and British reluctance to quit its naval base in Malta. Bonaparte finally declared war and stated his intention of invading and occupying England.

Along the Channel and Atlantic ports he had constructed 2000 flat-bottomed barges to carry his Grand Army with floating fortresses to protect them while crossing the straits to Dover and other English beaches. On the Normandy coast and around Boulogne, he had massed 160,000 men under five of his best generals, Soult, Ney, Lannes, Junot and Davoust. Now, in the spring of 1803, he was waiting only for favourable weather. Pitt had returned to continue what had become almost a personal vendetta with Bonaparte.

'Do you really think he can do it, William?' Addington asked.

'I don't think anybody else could,' Pitt answered, implying that Bonaparte might succeed.

'And to think we took him prisoner and let him go,' Dundas lamented, sliding his snuffbox along the table.

He was referring to Bonaparte's escape from Egypt after Nelson had destroyed the French fleet at the Battle of the Nile. Secret orders had gone to Nelson to let Bonaparte's ship, the frigate *Muiron*, through the blockade; at that point, Bonaparte had given the British authorities verbal assurances that when he had overthrown the five-man

Directory which ruled France he would make peace with England and keep France within her natural frontiers. Instead, he had set Europe ablaze with wars of conquest and revolutionary ideas and openly declared his ambition to bring the old enemy, England, to her knees and embark on world domination.

Silence fell over the table as the four men reflected on Bonaparte's incredible ascendancy and the fabulous achievements that gave him a superhuman character.

Addington flicked a glance at Pitt, thinking what an old man he looked at forty-four. Those war years had taken their toll. So had his heavy and increasing consumption of port wine — though who could blame him for that? Certainly not he, Addington. Hadn't his own father, physician to the Pitt family, prescribed port for William, the frail boy, and thus started the addiction? All the same, Addington wondered how long his friend would last with those hollow cheeks fired by a tippler's flush, the trembling hand hooked round the heavy glass and the nervous twitch of his eyelids. How long, when he must soon answer the public call to resume office and fight another war against Bonaparte? Addington sensed that Pitt felt time running out on him and the country in this unending conflict.

'I wish he would drop dead,' Dundas muttered.

'If only Saint-Réjant had lit that fuse five seconds earlier two and a half years ago,' the fourth man put in.

William Windham shared the war office with Dundas and had helped organize and support several Chouan royalist armies in the western provinces of France. A fluent French speaker, his powdered wig, ruffed cravat, velvet coat and silk breeches made him look as elegant as the French *émigré* princes whom he numbered among his closest friends.

'That assassination attempt only strengthened the man's hand,' Dundas muttered. 'It turned him into a popular hero, and they'd have made him a martyr if Saint-Réjant had succeeded.'

'Who would they have put in his place'?' Addington asked. 'That's the question.'

'Not the Bourbons,' Dundas grunted. 'They made too big a mess of things, and anyway too many French politicians voted Louis XVI's death to invite his brothers back and face the guillotine themselves.'

Pitt remained silent, sipping his port and listening to the argument. He had convened this meeting at Downing Street, for although he held no government office, everyone in and out of Parliament considered him the real leader of the country and Addington no more than a caretaker. Hadn't Pitt's brilliant political disciple, George Canning, quipped, 'Pitt is to Addington, as London to Paddington.'

'I wouldn't rule out the Bourbons,' Pitt murmured. 'If we had one or two brilliant generals with a foot in both royalist and republican camps to prepare the return of the monarchy ... ' When the others looked askance, he went on, 'After all, we have here in London one of the most gifted of all revolutionary generals, the man who conquered Holland for the French republicans but would now like to see a king back on the throne.'

'Pichegru,' Dundas said and Pitt nodded. General Charles Pichegru, banished by the republicans to the penal colony of Devil's Island in French Guyana in 1797 for a royalist plot, had escaped and sought refuge in London four years before. His exploits, both as a general and a politician, had made his name a byword in France. 'And he'd be willing to tilt at Bonaparte?' Dundas asked, and again Pitt nodded. 'But you'd need somebody at the top of the army in Paris as well.'

Pitt nodded. 'What about Pichegru's old

second-in-command, General Jean-Victor Moreau?'

Dundas raised his eyebrows. 'You mean the General Moreau of . . . ' And he began to recite the verses of his fellow-Scotsman, Thomas Campbell, commemorating the Battle of Hohenlinden where Moreau, with superlative tactics, defeated a huge Austrian army in December 1800.

On Linden when the sun was low,
All bloodless lay the untrodden snow,
And dark as winter was the flow
Of Iser rolling rapidly.
But Linden saw another sight
When the drums beat at dead of night
Commanding fires of death to light
The darkness of her scenery . . .

'That's the man,' Pitt said. 'Windham will fill in the details later on, but royalists agents in Paris have told *émigré* leaders here that he has agreed to co-operate with Pichegru and the royalists to stage a *coup d'état* overthrowing Bonaparte and restoring the Bourbons.'

'And so we think Bonaparte will stand by and let those two generals take over Paris and the rest of the country?' Dundas asked.

'Bonaparte won't be there.'

'Oh! Where will he be?'

Without a word, Pitt rose and went to the world map hanging on the cabinet office wall. Resting a forefinger on a dot just off the Normandy coast marking the British island of Jersey, he said, 'To begin with, he'll be there.'

His finger travelled west along the Channel, down the French and Spanish coasts, round the bulge of West Africa to halt on a pinprick in the South Atlantic, marked in red like the British colonies scattered throughout the map. 'I think Saint Helena's far enough away for him,' Pitt said.

'But Saint Helena belongs to the East India Company,' Dundas objected. 'They use it as a staging post for their Indian tea clippers.'

'I expect we can persuade them to renounce their rights in the national interest,' Pitt murmured.

'With our command of the seas it's the perfect prison,' Windham interjected.

'So, we only have one problem — how to persuade Monsieur Napoleone Buonaparte to step aboard one of His Majesty's men-o'-war,' Dundas said, tongue-in-cheek, as he pushed the port decanter round the table. 'We've been talking about kidnapping that man for nearly three years, and nobody's any nearer.'

'Admitted,' Pitt said.

Just after the Austrian defeat at Marengo in

1800, the royalist leader Guillaume Hyde de Neuville had arrived in London with a plan to kill or kidnap Bonaparte but, at at that time, no one in Pitt's government seriously contemplated such a plot, believing Bonaparte would make peace and prepare the return of the monarchy. But Bonaparte had snubbed Louis XVI's successor, declaring he would do everything to prevent a return to the old regime; moreover, he had held on to territories in Belgium and Holland that threatened England's security and trade.

'Our situation has changed since Hyde de Neuville proposed his plan,' Pitt went on. 'Bonaparte is only twenty-one miles away with more than a hundred and fifty thousand men and an invasion fleet, and he won't stop until he has destroyed us. In any case, Addington will confirm that even a short war will bankrupt us.'

'William is right,' Addington said. 'We can no longer afford to subsidize any European armies — or even the royalists in Brittany and on the Rhine.'

'So we think No Bonaparte No War,' Dundas said.

'Exactly,' Pitt said. 'It would save hundreds of thousands of lives and a lot of misery and money if we could get rid of Bonaparte.'

'Get rid of Bonaparte?' Dundas said.

'I mean, ship him off to Saint Helena and let the navy look after him for the rest of his life.' Pitt paused to look at his three companions, now intent on his words. 'Of course, if it so happens that he resists and more force than necessary is used and he is killed we shall have to consider him as a casualty of war.'

'Do we have a plan for this?' Addington asked.

'We have, but I am not at liberty to tell you what it is,' Pitt replied. 'All I can say is that it will cost us more than a million pounds in gold coin and letters of exchange.'

'A million pounds!' Addington gasped.

Pitt merely shrugged. 'We've squandered more in a few weeks on beaten European armies,' he said. 'And you can reckon how long a million pounds will last if we have to fight Bonaparte on our own. You merely have to draw that sum from secret funds and let Windham and myself have it by this time next week.'

'And you say you don't know how it will be used,' Addington persisted.

'No, and I don't want to know,' Pitt said. 'All I may reveal is that the man who claims he can abduct Bonaparte and hand him over to us is the only man we think capable of carrying out his promise. You'd agree with that, Windham?'

'He's one of the finest and bravest men I have ever met,' Windham said.

'Is he honest?' Addington, the puritan, queried.

'Too honest, perhaps,' Windham replied.

'Do we know him?' Dundas asked.

'For us he is only a *nom de guerre*,' Pitt said. 'We know him only as Gideon.'

3

A few nights later, Pitt strolled the fifty yards from his mansion in York Place to the new house at 14 Baker Street occupied by the Count of Artois. At the entrance to the short drive, Windham was waiting with a carriage and liveried footmen, for the count, descendant of Saint Louis, brother of Louis XVI and second in line to the French throne, would have raised an eyebrow at a British political leader who arrived on foot without the proper escort.

When the two British statesmen had followed a footman in yellow livery along a corridor and into the ballroom, Pitt had the curious impression of intruding on some fancy-dress ball or period play. Or stepping back fifty years into some privileged corner of Versailles Palace.

In an alcove, an orchestra of three violins, a cello, two flutes and an oboe was playing a minuet to which cavaliers and their ladies were dancing solemnly. Their footwork, postures and formal gestures reminded Pitt of so many marionettes who appeared as outmoded as their costumes, most of the men wore brocaded coats and waistcoats, silk breeches and stockings, lace jabots and sleeves and silver-buckled shoes; their partners had silk dresses with ribbed bodices and ballooning skirts over hooped wires or stiffened petticoats; their hair they had tiered and powdered in the old style while the men wore powdered wigs.

Artois himself came to greet the two British leaders, whispering to Pitt, 'The person you have come to meet has not yet arrived.' He moved back to his seat among his retinue.

Pitt had little time for Artois, or indeed for most of the aristocrats who formed his court. So many of them lived the illusion that the day after tomorrow they would return to France to resume their leisured and sybaritic existence which a nightmare or mental aberration called the French Revolution had so pointlessly interrupted. Artois personified this notion. Two days after the Bastille fell in July 1789, he had fled, first of the royal émigrés to quit France.

He would return, he assured everybody, when the brouhaha had died down and France had regained her senses in a few months; now, fifteen footloose years later, he remained in exile having seen his brother the king, guillotined in January 1793 and with him thousands of aristocrats, the flower of French nobility.

During those years, he had done virtually nothing to win back the Bourbon throne, frittering his time away with his mistress, Louise de Polastron, or at the whist table rather than risk his neck. Pitt wished he had followed the example of his cousin, the young Duc d'Enghien, who had fought bravely and brilliantly to regain France for his dynasty and even now waited on the Rhine for a chance to lead an army back into his own country and overthrow the republic.

As the two Englishmen watched the minuet change to a gavotte, Artois's young son, the Duc de Berri, crossed the room to shake Windham's hand and bow to Pitt. A tall, heavy-set man with lugubrious eyes accompanied him. 'May I present Monsieur Mehée de la Touche,' the young duke said, 'He's a writer who has been acting as one of our agents in France, but they arrested someone who betrayed him and he had to flee.'

'Your authorities detained me on Jersey thinking I was a republican spy.' Mehée grinned, showing rotten teeth that contrasted with his elegant dress coat and satin waistcoat.

'How are things in France?' Windham asked.

'Bonaparte has spies everywhere in case somebody tries to stage a *coup d'état*.'

'A royalist *coup d'état*?' Windham prompted, flicking a glance at Pitt.

'Oh, there are several republican generals who have their eye on the Tuileries as well,' Mehée murmured. 'Our beloved First Consul doesn't even trust his own generals and goes in terror of assassination.'

'Then why has he just sacked the finest policeman and spymaster in France?' Pitt interjected.

'You mean, Fouché?' Mehée produced a snuffbox, took a pinch and sneezed genteelly. 'Talleyrand poisoned Bonaparte's ear by saying Fouché was concocting royalist and Jacobin plots to foil them and take the credit.'

'Bonaparte didn't swallow that story?' Pitt said.

'No — the real reason is that Fouché knew too much about Bonaparte and his Corsican clan and might have blocked Bonaparte's road to the throne.'

'The throne!'

'Well, now he's just caesar. And my royalist and republican informants in Paris believe he will crown himself king or emperor when he invents the right pretext.' Mehée paused to fix the two statesmen with his muddy black eyes. 'That's why the royalists here and in

46

France must act now or never.'

'What do you mean — act?'

Mehée chopped with the edge of his hand across the nape of his neck. 'The revolutionaries threw the head of Louis XVI at the royalists and the rest of Europe as a challenge and a warning of what they could expect. We should do the same on our side.'

'An interesting notion,' Pitt murmured 'Are you going to volunteer for the task of disposing of the First Consul?'

Mehée gave a gap-toothed grin, held out a scrawny hand and said, 'Put half a million golden louis there and give me thirty determined men and I think I could promise results.'

'Have you put your scheme to the Count of Artois?' Windham asked.

'When he's over his wig in debt?'

Pitt knew only too well Artois could hardly finance his own extravagance let alone mount a raid into France to murder Bonaparte; for three years he had lived in the royal palace of Holyroodhouse in Edinburgh, never daring to show his face in daylight, for under a law permitting arrest only in daylight he would have found himself in a debtors' jail.

Pitt looked at Mehée then said, drily, 'I would advise you to forget such hare-brained schemes.'

Bowing to the Frenchman, he moved to the drinks table. There, he sipped a glass of claret while taking stock of the company. Idly, he wondered how long Artois's mistress would last with that tell-tale flush on both cheeks. Rumour whispered she had Artois under her thumb and had prevented him from raising an army to fight for the French monarchy. A romantic thesis. Pitt believed a more basic emotion blocked Artois's action — self-preservation fuelled by funk.

Suddenly Windham nudged him and pointed to the impressive figure who had entered the room and gone to bow to Artois.

'Cadoudal,' he whispered.

Now Pitt realized why this yeoman's son from Brittany had thrust upwards through the old guard of aristocrats to assume command of the Chouan armies in his native province and La Vendée. With his mere appearance, General Georges Cadoudal seemed to bring all these dummies of the *ancien régime* alive.

His presence filled the room. He stood a full head taller than everybody, but it was his broad face and bull neck, the span of his shoulders and broad thighs that gave him the appearance of a colossus. He wore no wig, which anyway would have looked incongruous on a massive head covered with reddish, curly hair. His burly torso seemed about to rip open the cummerbund, frock coat and breeches he was wearing. Across the coat, a red cordon made a diagonal slash, and Pitt recognized this as the Order of Saint Louis, a rare honour. He noticed one other thing: how these fragile, thoroughbred ladies turned sly and covetous eyes on him, and how he ignored them all.

'He looks like Hercules,' Pitt whispered to Windham.

'He acts like him, too,' the minister replied. 'He's one of the few royalists with the stature to do great things.'

Pitt had already learned something of Georges Cadoudal's exploits as leader of the Chouans, the most fervent royalists in France; for seven years, this Herculean figure had symbolized royalist resistance to the revolution.

After Pitt had backed an expeditionary force in 1795 only to watch it crushed at Quiberon in Brittany, Cadoudal had gathered the rags of the Chouan army and reformed and revitalized them; he had established a network of royalist units stretching from Cape Finisterre through Paris to Lyon and even into Provence. As a guerrilla leader he had no equal; as an army commander leading nearly 20,000 men he had punished a strong republican force at Pont de Loc, forcing the government to keep large garrisons throughout western France. No one disputed his place as the most able of royalist generals.

Pitt and Windham overheard Artois say to his general, 'My son, the Duc de Berri, tells me he noticed you in Hyde Park the other day, General Cadoudal, but you did not acknowledge him.'

'Had he been with soldiers instead of fancy ladies, I would have saluted him,' Cadoudal replied.

One of Artois's circle sneered, then said, 'His Highness, the Duc de Berri will only have to set foot in Brittany to rally every man to his cause.'

'Then why doesn't he come?' Cadoudal said, loudly, and Pitt observed his neck veins balloon with anger as he uttered the remark. Artois parried his criticism with a wave of his hand and Cadoudal took his leave with a curt bow. Spotting Windham, he crossed the room to shake his hand.

'We had a meeting tonight,' Windham whispered.

'Not here,' Cadoudal murmured. 'Too many people we cannot trust. Wait.'

Half an hour later, a scrawny, craggy-faced individual in shabby livery and an unpowdered wig approached and beckoned them to follow him; he had a cabriolet waiting and quickly whipped the horses into motion through the quiet streets. At New Bond Street, he stopped at Number Six.

Cadoudal greeted them at the entrance to the three upstairs rooms he used as his headquarters, explaining he had sent his aide, Captain Le Ridant to fetch them for security reasons. 'I don't trust men like that newcomer, Mehée de la Touche,' he muttered.

In this small, low-ceilinged room, he appeared even more massive. 'What will you drink — cognac or claret?' he asked, pointing to the magnum bottles on his sideboard.

Noting Pitt's eyebrows arch at the French liquor that he had taxed heavily when Englishmen could procure it, Cadoudal grinned. 'You forget the Chouan rebellion began with smugglers who didn't like paying republican taxes,' he said. 'So, don't ask if I have paid duty on these.' His Breton French burred like Henry Dundas's English. Pouring only two drops into the bottom of his own glass, he raised it and proclaimed, 'Here's to the downfall of the tyrant.'

'We have allocated the funds,' Pitt murmured, then after a pause, he added, 'But of course, we'd like to have some idea of what you intend doing with them.'

'Simple,' Cadoudal grunted. 'Get rid of Bonaparte and put Louis XVIII where he belongs, on the French throne.'

'We meant your plan of action, Georges,' Windham put in.

'Ah, that!' Cadoudal cried. 'Only a handful of people know my plan and that's how it should be.'

'Surely you don't propose to stage a *coup d'état* and kidnap Bonaparte with only a handful of people,' Pitt remarked.

Cadoudal looked at them and shrugged. 'I already have several hundred men in the capital who shall know enough of my plans to come together at the right moment. And in Brittany and La Vendée I have more than twenty thousand armed men ready to march on Paris at a word from me.'

'But Bonaparte is the key figure,' Pitt insisted. 'Surely you have a separate plan for him.'

'I've thought of nothing but that plan for more than two years,' Cadoudal growled, smacking a huge fist into his open palm to emphasize the statement.

'I have more than one score to settle with that little Corsican upstart.'

'And you can deliver him?'

'All you have to do is have a ship on the coast to take him aboard.'

'Half the fleet if necessary,' Pitt said.

This young general's hatred of Bonaparte might run deep, but no deeper than his own. He might not live to see this long war won, but might at least witness the beginning of the end if this Cadoudal brought off what he called his Vital Strike and abducted or killed Bonaparte.

'General Cadoudal, you've met Bonaparte, haven't you?'

'Near enough to kill him.'

'How did he impress you?'

'A funny little man with straggling hair in a general's uniform far too big for him, who spoke with an Italian twang and listened only to himself,' Cadoudal said. He paused, his mouth tightening at the recollection of the hour he had spent with the First Consul at the Tuileries, when he had tried to buy him off with bribes of money and honours and a command. All he had to do was swear allegiance to Bonaparte and the republic. All! His face suffused with blood and his hands clenched. 'I felt like wrapping my fingers round his little neck and throttling him,' Cadoudal shouted. 'He's a dictator who won't rest until he's a king unless we stop him.'

'So many people have tried but nobody has succeeded,' Windham said, sipping his claret.

'Ah, but this time he won't be able to halt a revolution by mowing down good Frenchmen on church steps with grapeshot; he'll be on the way to the coast, or — '

'Or dead,' Pitt interjected.

'He put a price on my head, alive or dead, three years ago,' Cadoudal replied. 'If Bonaparte and his guard resist, we shall have no choice but to kill them.' He paused before adding, 'After all, we're at war and his republican soldiers have killed hundreds of thousands of loyal Frenchmen and good Europeans in the name of peace, liberty and justice.'

'You have your faithful Chouans, but can you be certain the generals, Pichegru and Moreau, will rally the royalists and doubtful republicans to the Bourbons?' Pitt asked.

'Moreau I do not know, but Pichegru I would trust with my life.'

'And which of the princes?'

'Monsieur le Prince, or his son, the Duc de Berri — it doesn't matter which of them as long as they can assure Louis XVIII of a triumphal return to Paris.'

'And you really think Artois or Berri will come and lead your *coup d'état*,' Pitt asked, a dubious ring in his voice.

Cadoudal looked gravely at both men then strode to his desk to seize a small, leather-bound Bible, its covers and pages grimy and obviously well-thumbed. On this he placed his hand and intoned, loudly, 'I swear by my God, my name and my rank, by everything I hold sacred that you shall see one of the princes by our side on the great day.'

As though overcome with the emotion of that statement, he escorted the two statesmen to the door and said a curt goodnight.

Pitt and Windham wandered down New Bond Street, crossed Piccadilly to St James's Street and the Goosetree Club for a nightcap. Dundas rose from the card table and joined them in a quiet corner. 'Well, did you meet our Breton avenging angel?' he said with a grin. 'Has he any chance of bringing us back Bonaparte, alive or dead?'

'I don't know,' Pitt answered, 'but I'm willing to back him to the tune of a million pounds to find out.'

'Windham, you know him best,' Dundas said. 'What makes you think he can pull off this coup?'

'In a word — God,' Windham replied. 'He genuinely believes that God will arm his hand to destroy this anti-Christ called Bonaparte.'

'A good few million respected Christians have prayed long and deep for a speedy end to the First Consul without much luck,'

Dundas grunted. 'I don't like men with too many lofty ideals or loyalties. Give me the venal man every time.'

'Henry has something there,' Pitt murmured. 'I must say I prefer professional men who work for money, or power, or women.'

'He does have a young lady he loves,' Windham said.

'Ah! That's more like it,' Dundas said.

'But he's a virgin, like her, so they assure me.'

'A virgin!' Dundas echoed, incredulously, looking askance at Pitt, then raising his eyebrows as though implying his doubt about the existence of virginity altogether.

'They've plighted their troth but have promised to put any thought of marriage out of their heads until the king has regained his throne.'

Dundas filled three glasses from the decanter of port he had ordered. 'Seems a quaint fellow,' he muttered. 'But I'll drink to him and his mission — and let's hope we'll all soon be invited to his wedding.'

At that, the three statesmen raised their glasses and drank the toast.

4

Cadoudal spun his horse round and hoisted his stave to deflect the blow from the charging rider who aimed a stave at his head. With little more than a flick of his wrist, Cadoudal twisted the man round, hurled him to the ground and pinned him there on the end of his stave. Leaning down, he helped Armand Gaillard to his feet then patiently showed the fair-haired Norman youth how to point his stave for the charge, how to parry and cut when fighting hand-to-hand with cavalrymen.

His lesson in swordsmanship finished, he toured the tented camp set up in the forest between Romsey and Winchester. About fifty men, mostly Chouan officers, were doing combat training with sheathed English cavalry swords, either mounted or on foot; a dozen were practising in a clearing with muskets and pistols; a rawboned figure with a face pitted from powder burns was teaching another group how to handle a pistol and dagger, as well as cruder forms of unarmed combat.

Cadoudal grimaced at the clumsy way

these men handled firearms. But what did one expect from Breton farmers and sailors? Seizing a brace of pistols from one man, he cocked them and aimed at the small dummy slung from a branch then fired both barrels together; one bullet opened a gaping rent in the head while the other penetrated just beneath the heart. 'That's how good they've got to be, Pierre,' he said.

'They'll be ready when you are,' Pierre Guillemot replied. One of Cadoudal's oldest comrades, he had fought in every Chouan war and, though only a peasant farmer, even republicans called him the King of Bignan, his native Breton region which he ruled like royalty.

A rider galloped into the clearing and signalled to another man who was waiting to take up the relay and immediately spurred his horse in the direction of Winchester. Guillemot glanced at his silver hunter. 'That's a hundred miles in six hours changing horses every ten miles.'

'Get it down to five hours,' Cadoudal said.

'With good Breton horses instead of these hacks we'll do two hundred miles a day.'

Cadoudal looked at him, wondering why he had mentioned 200 miles — the distance between Paris and the Normandy coast. Guillemot knew about the *coup d'état* but not about the abduction of Bonaparte, or why they were thrashing their horses and running a coach between Romsey and Winchester in relays of ten and twenty miles.

Nobody knew his whole plan, just as nobody could prove he had sent Saint-Réjant to Paris to destroy Bonaparte. And if that little gnome had failed in the Rue Saint-Nicaise through lack of foresight, he would not fail.

Piece by piece, he had assembled his plan and now stood at the centre of a complex web which he could now begin to tighten around the First Consul. People like Pitt, Windham and even Artois had garnered no more than fragments of the plot, for Cadoudal realized a chance word or a slip would lead him and his small army straight to the guillotine.

'Nobody stepped out of line?' he asked. Guillemot admitted two men had spent a night in Romsey with loose women, and another two had gone absent for three days to spend their pay on rough cider in Winchester. Cadoudal gave all four men a tongue-lashing and repeated his orders: No drink and no women. He fined each three months' pay and confined them to camp for a month.

For soldiers, celibacy and sobriety seemed alien orders, but Cadoudal ran his army like

Loyola his Jesuits, or Cromwell his Round-
heads; he felt the pangs of sexual continence
himself at times, but women were as
dangerous as drink for a band of conspirators
and he never trusted those who liked either or
both too much.

'You have six months to pull these men
into shape and join me in Paris,' he told
Guillemot. 'When I leave in two weeks' time
you deal through Captain Fridainque for pay,
rations and equipment, or through the
English general, Holder.'

'Six more months in this God-forsaken
land,' Guillemot groaned.

'You're speaking of the English who have
fed, lodged and clothed us and are our only
hope of returning to France for good,'
Cadoudal barked.

'Sorry, Georges,' Guillemot said. 'Are you
having *soupe* with us for the last time?'

As Cadoudal nodded, a horseman rode
into the clearing, dismounted and approached.
Taller even than Cadoudal, he had a
powerful, limber figure and the face and
bearing of someone used to command.

'Captain Fridainque will have *soupe* too,'
Cadoudal told Guillemot. 'Send Louis Picot
to our tent when it's ready.'

To the newcomer, Cadoudal outlined their
progress since the previous meeting; they had

taken his advice and adopted the English cavalry sabre for the cut and thrust of hand-to-hand fighting rather than the straight French sword; they had ordered English dragoon-guards uniforms, which were the nearest resemblance to Bonaparte's consular guard to rehearse their combats; they had relay teams training every day to make the trip from Paris to the Channel coast with a double burden.

Fridainque listened then said, 'Don't forget you'll be making that trip in darkness and maybe through snow and ice.'

'I've picked two dozen of our best men and they'll get through.'

Even the king's general, Cadoudal, deferred to this captain. Not because of his seniority but because the name, Captain Fridainque, camouflaged one of the most celebrated and remarkable of all French revolutionary generals: Charles Pichegru.

An extraordinary man, Pichegru. Ten years older than Cadoudal, he matched him in height if not in strength and outshone him intellectually. As a general in his twenties, he had commanded the republican army, which had conquered Holland; he had set the whole of France talking about his cavalry charge across the frozen Zuider Zee to capture the Dutch fleet, locked in the ice.

At the height of his fame, he became president of the revolutionary representative body, but in 1797 his career finished in disgrace and exile. He was accused by Bonaparte and others of plotting to restore the Bourbons and attempting to suborn the National Assembly by a royalist coup.

Shipped to the penal settlement of Devil's Island in French Guyana, he might have mouldered and died like most of his fellow convicts, but Pichegru plotted his escape and led seven of his companions on an epic 300 mile journey through cruel jungle and swamp to be rescued, more dead than alive, by a British frigate.

When he had fought off yellow fever he made his way to London where he impressed leading statesmen like Pitt and Thomas Paine, author of *The Rights of Man*. Soon, he was listening to Artois, who persuaded him to throw his weight behind Cadoudal's plot.

Pichegru had become a key figure for another reason: his former second-in-command, General Jean-Victor Moreau, had an immense following in Paris and the provinces among republican troops, and even Bonaparte viewed him as a rival and threat to his rule. If Pichegru and Moreau came together, they could rally enough royalist and republican troops to take over the capital and proclaim the restored monarchy as soon as Cadoudal had dealt with Bonaparte. So ran the thinking of Artois and other leading *émigrés*.

Although Pichegru lived in Brompton Row, ten minutes through Hyde Park and Kensington Gardens from Cadoudal's rooms, both men preferred to meet in Winchester forest; they well knew Fouché and the French Ambassador General Antoine-François Andréossy, had planted spies everywhere in *émigré* circles. Just how closely those spies were watching them they saw from the official French Government gazette, *Le Moniteur*, which arrived regularly. In fact, Pichegru had brought one of the latest copies and handed it to Cadoudal, who read:

In London. Georges (Cadoudal) openly wears his Cordon Rouge as a reward for the infernal machine which destroyed a Parisian district and killed 30 women, children and citizens. From this special favour we can assume that, had he succeeded, they would have given him the Order of the Garter.

'Only one man could have dictated that — Bonaparte,' Pichegru murmured, putting

63

the paper in his pocket. 'It means he has linked you with the Saint-Nicaise bomb plot.'

'It was an open secret.'

They understood each other, the Breton and the man from the eastern province of Franche-Comté. Both owed their education to priests; both had come up through the ranks, from private to general; both had kept the royalist faith and wished to see their king restored and their country rid of revolution and war.

In Cadoudal's tent they settled on crude stools. Pichegru lit his pipe and savoured a glass of smuggled brandy. 'How many men are you taking next week?' he asked.

'Only six, to fix billets and caches for the others and test the relay stations from Paris to the coast.'

'We're now in August,' Pichegru mused, 'that gives us six months to prepare.' They had planned the coup for mid-winter; reasoning that Paris would turn out unwillingly on a cold night to save Bonaparte, and the empty streets would allow royalists and republican defectors room for manoeuvre.

Louis Picot, the Breton general's orderly, brought them the meat and vegetable stew the men were having as their evening meal. A swarthy little man, ugly as an ape with a long, mournful face, he doled their stew into mess-tins and gave them each a fork and spoon. Cadoudal gestured at his retreating figure. 'I'm taking him.'

'A bit dangerous, that. Wasn't he with Saint-Réjant as an orderly?'

'Yes, but he had no part in the gunpowder plot.'

'No matter; Fouché will have him on his books and might connect everything if he's caught.'

'But Fouché has been sacked.'

'Don't wager on that. Bonaparte doesn't trust him and prefers to be his own chief policeman. But I know Fouché and he never gives up. His own paid spies are everywhere.'

'You know Bonaparte as well as anybody, what sort of policeman will he make?'

For several minutes, Pichegru pondered that question. His mind backtracked twenty-four years to the day when, at 18, he was acting as a lay teacher at the Château de Brienne in eastern France and they brought a 10-year-old Corsican boy there to prepare for the École Militaire. Even in his polyglot mixture of Italian, French and Corsican argot, that slip of a boy, Napoleone Buonaparte had held his own with the aristocratic and upper-crust youths who mocked him as a low-born alien, as a Corsican with a quaint accent, manners and shabby dress. Stubborn, proud, ambitious, fearless, indefatigable, yes and highly intelligent — Pichegru remembered that schoolboy as all of those things.

What a curious mind he had! It mopped up tracts of Justinian and Plutarch and Tacitus and vomited them verbatim, yet a village halfwit could have given him points in French spelling which he learned laboriously; no one, then or now, doubted his flair for mathematics which had taken him into Pichegru's own branch of the services — artillery. Bonaparte calculated everything, leaving nothing to chance; he was ruthless, devious. Pichegru also remembered that Bonaparte's ancestors came from Florence, home of Machiavelli and the Borgias.

'I would think Bonaparte has every quality of a brilliant policeman,' he replied, finally. 'Never underestimate him.'

'I often wonder what made a little man like that a successful general?'

Pichegru pushed aside his stew and stuffed tobacco into his pipe as he reflected. 'You've met him yourself,' he said. 'You must have noticed his gift of winning people over, making them his. All his men, and even his generals adore him. Then he has the genius for bringing off the brilliant and unexpected manoeuvre in everything he does. Always expect the unexpected from Bonaparte, and never look for him to do the same thing twice running. Now, if he'd been on time for the opera that night two and a half years ago . . . '

Both men fell silent. Cadoudal thought of how bravely the little nobleman, Saint-Réjant, had gone to the guillotine. Would he be as courageous if he failed in his plan to kidnap or kill Bonaparte?

Pichegru was considering the scores he had to settle with the First Consul. As an unknown general, the Corsican had turned his guns on a hungry crowd on the steps of Saint-Roch church to crush a revolt on orders of the Directory. Pichegru had openly condemned this massacre and Bonaparte had never forgiven him; he had paid him out by producing captured papers and denouncing Pichegru's relations with the Bourbon princes.

'They say he's lucky.'

'Oh, he has courage, too,' Pichegru said. 'You've heard the advice an old sweat gave a new recruit who asked how he could become a colonel. 'Do your damnedest to get yourself killed and if you don't succeed they'll make you a general.' Bonaparte did just that; he has that sort of courage.'

'He's won a lot of his glory through the graveyard.'

'Maybe, but he's clever, fighting his glory battles abroad, and burying French dead there, and at home he draws the teeth of both the royalists and extreme republicans.'

'You mean by allowing *émigrés* to return and promising them their estates: they'll never see them.'

'No, but it makes the First Consul look like a liberal statesman.'

'And a hypocrite who wants to look like a good Catholic,' Cadoudal cried. 'Filling Nôtre-Dame with his anti-Christ followers and forcing the Pope to agree to reinstate the faith in France.'

'A brilliant tactical move,' Pichegru retorted. 'Think of the recruits it costs us among priests and the faithful.'

Cadoudal was forced to agree. Bonaparte had made a Concordat with the Vatican, and this had broken much of the resistance in pious towns and villages in Brittany, Normandy and La Vendée; many of his best soldiers had surrendered their arms, and thousands of priests had returned to their churches, believing in the First Consul's sincerity.

'God is with us,' Cadoudal cried, as though to convince himself. Pichegru shrugged, biting his tongue on the remark that God had curious ways of manifesting his support. Up to now Bonaparte and the Devil had triumphed.

Under the beech trees on that sultry August day, the two generals ran over the final plan. When Cadoudal had tested their lifeline route to and from Paris, he would build up hundreds of royalist cells in the capital and strengthen them with detachments from this camp; he would prepare the attack on Bonaparte and seek a safe house for the princes. But he promised to do nothing until Pichegru arrived during the winter with one or both princes. At that moment, they would strike in the capital and the western provinces.

Before parting company, the Breton requested one of the priests to hold an open-air mass for the group. A devout man, Pichegru took part in the Latin ceremony. He observed that, in the responses and hymns, Cadoudal's bull voice resounded above all the others; his acceptance of the bread and wine, symbols of the body and blood of Christ, struck the older general as one of the most humble acts he had ever witnessed.

Then everything about Cadoudal intrigued him; his faith and ascetic life — his sobriety and sexual abstinence, his courage and commanding personality. With anyone else, Pichegru would have scoffed at the notion of a *coup d'état* coupled with kidnapping or killing Bonaparte, but something about this young Breton suggested he might bring off the gamble; even his blind faith had infected Pichegru.

Anyway, he had sat on the sidelines too long, and Cadoudal's plan attracted him by its very boldness. In any event, how could he sit watching the seasons come and go in Kensington Gardens while men like this Chouan were fighting for their ideals, while these men in training around them were chancing their arm by returning to France, even if they had not aimed to overthrow the government?

At the end of the mass, Pichegru collected his belongings. He embraced Cadoudal. 'You know if we're caught we can expect only one thing.'

Cadoudal shrugged his huge shoulders. 'If God wills it that way, I shall accept my fate without flinching.'

'I shall see you in France.'

'I'll be there to meet you — but be sure to bring the princes with you.'

5

On the morning 18 August, 1803, Georges Cadoudal packed and stored his royalist uniform then dressed like a good republican in wide-lapelled jacket, cord breeches, leather calf-length boots. Round his neck, he knotted a silk cravat and on his head he placed a beaver hat. He packed a bag with a change of clothing, hiding within it a stiletto, a Highland dirk given him by his friend Captain John Wright, and the double-barelled flintlock pistol he had used throughout the Chouan wars.

His aide, Le Ridant, waited for him in the cab they had hired to take them to Hastings. He had already sent his small group there by the regular stagecoach. At one point, he had considered asking Pitt to have him set down, alone, on the west coast of Brittany to make his own way to Paris, but had decided to go with his small group.

Now, as they broke free from London, the fields of ripening corn and wheat, the sheep and cows round the hamlets and farms reminded him of his own farm at Kerléano, except everything here seemed so peaceful as

71

though the English peasants had never heard of war.

He longed for a glimpse of the rolling country round Lorient and Vannes with its calvaries and cairns, its islands lying like some mirage on the shimmering ocean. He had another yearning — to see the girl he loved, Lucrèce Mercier. For three years he had dreamed of her, had longed for a sight of her, had prayed for her. But he had resisted the impulse to go and see her. How could he trust himself to meet her in his own country and not weaken? He was returning to make a king and kill a tyrant; for that he would need all his courage, all his resolution. He had still another reason: he must check what he had dubbed the Liberty Line from Paris to the coast and ensure that Charles d'Hozier and his friend, Bouvet de Lozier, had found safe royalist families to shelter them and their valuable hostage.

Entering Hastings, six mounted troopers stopped their cab. A captain studied their papers and said, 'I regret, Monsieur Larive, you are under arrest.' He waved aside Cadoudal's protests and escorted their coach to the town hall where the six other members of the group sat in a locked room guarded by four soldiers.

'They think we're captured French sailors

who have escaped and are making their way back to France,' the Chevalier Edouard de la Haye Saint-Hilaire told him.

'What have you said to them?'

'Nothing,' Saint-Hilaire replied. 'That is . . . well, I'd better tell you: Querelle said something about our fighting for the English.'

'He said what?' Cadoudal growled.

'I don't think they believed him,' Saint-Hilaire whispered.

They had resigned themselves to spending a night in the town hall when their door burst open and a tall figure in naval officer's cutaway coat and knee-breeches entered and came to grasp Cadoudal's hand. 'I heard they'd captured a French giant and six escaped prisoners and thought I'd find you here,' he said.

Captain John Wesley Wright spoke French fluently. For five years he had ferried men and supplies from England to Brittany until the Chouans looked upon him as one of themselves. Wright also knew the inside of the Temple, grimmest of Parisian prisons. With his uncle, Sir Sidney Smith and Colonel Antoine de Philippeaux. A classmate of Bonaparte at Brienne, he had been chasing French privateers in the Channel in 1796 when they were captured and imprisoned in the Temple dungeons. By bribing the guards and enlisting royalist friends, Philippeaux and the two English sailors escaped. Three years later, Sir Sidney Smith and Philippeaux led a force which halted Bonaparte at Saint-Jean d'Acre when he marched from Egypt intending to seize Syria, crush Turkey then follow Alexander's route into India to break British domination in Asia.

Wright talked them free then bundled them and their belongings into coaches to take them to the harbour where his cutter, the *Bonnetat*, was lying. Before they left the town hall, Cadoudal called over Jean-Pierre Querelle. 'You're not coming,' he said.

'But why, *mon général?*'

'You blabbed to the British and you'll do the same if you're caught by the republicans.'

'Never, *mon général*. Are not the British our allies?'

'You had orders to say nothing. You could have ruined the whole expedition.'

Querelle drew up his short figure and placed his right hand on his heart. 'I swear by God and all that I hold dear I shall never open my mouth again,' he said. 'Forgive me, *mon général.*'

Cadoudal gazed at the pinched, pock-marked face. This man had never fought with the Chouans but had fled to England merely to evade his creditors. No one who jeopardized the mission could expect leniency. Cadoudal had made the rule and should follow it. But Querelle had once served as a naval surgeon and time and again had proved his medical skill. And he, Cadoudal, the Chouan Hercules, had to admit he was a hypochondriac. He was betraying his own weakness, breaking his own code.

'All right,' he said, loud enough for everyone to hear, 'but next time I'll cut your tongue out.'

Watching the others come over the side of the *Bonnetat*, he had no qualms about cowardice or treachery. Every man had proved his valour a hundred times over. His adjutant, Aimé Joyaux, for instance. He had taken part in the Saint-Nicaise bomb plot, but had slipped through Fouché's cordon around Paris before the capture of Saint-Réjant and Carbon. Fearless as a lion and as skilled as his general with dagger and pistol, he bounded on to the deck.

'*Eh bien, mon général*, we'll be back home tonight,' Joyaux said.

Cadoudal shook his head, pointing to the fog drifting across the harbour.

Now, Jean-Baptiste Coster-Saint-Victor came aboard. From his frizzy hair on which his coiffeur lavished hours, through his ruffed shirt and silk breeches down to his gem-studded shoe-buckles, Coster looked a dandy or a fop. Only Cadoudal and a few other Chouans knew what courage lay under that languid and haughty mask. Coster, too, had helped assemble the Saint-Nicaise bomb, hoping to take to the streets with his royalists after Bonaparte's death. He had fled to America, but on his return had told Cadoudal, 'I would dearly like to finish the job on that scoundrel.'

Louis Picot appeared over the gunwale, monkey face framed by his general's baggage. Picot could hardly scribe his own name and spoke halting French peppered with his native Breton phrases. Faith in God, love of his king and loyalty to his officers had impelled him to forsake his family and follow Saint-Réjant then Cadoudal. Picot had little inkling of where they were going let alone their purpose. Even if he had, he would never talk.

Edouard de la Haye Saint-Hilaire's mop of blond hair showed over the ship's side. Commander of an élite battalion in 1799 when Cadoudal's Chouans had crushed republican forces under General Harty at Pont de Loc, he, too, had played some part in the Saint-Réjant plot and had fled to America. In the capital and western provinces, he knew hundreds of royalist officers ready to unearth their arms at his signal. Scores of Saint-Hilaire's relations and friends had perished on the guillotine during Robespierre's Reign of Terror. Nothing blunted his humour. 'Isn't Hastings where we Frenchmen landed in the first place?' he said. 'So, we're returning the compliment.'

On the *Bonnetat* they met Jean-Pierre Herpely and Gaston Troche who had returned from Normandy with John Wright to guide them to their first relay post. Before they weighed anchor, Cadoudal assembled his small band on deck and offered up a prayer for the success of their mission while English sailors in their striped jerseys, bell-bottoms, bare feet and with their hair ending in tarry pigtails, gazed at the ceremony being held in the curious Breton tongue.

Wright's cutter would take them in close to the shore; he had made the crossing so many times he could smell every shoal and knew every current. Now, groping through the fog, he drifted north then set course for the French coast below Dieppe. At Tréport, they slid round a French patrol then had to spend the whole of 22 August standing off, waiting for the fog to lift and allow them to land under night cover.

Their longboat found a deserted stretch of cliff near Biville and their luck held; some smugglers had constructed an *estamperche*, a thick rope slung between stakes punched into the sheer cliff face. Hand over hand, the Chouans pulled themselves the 150 feet to the top.

Cadoudal went last, and nearly got no further. With no one below him to hold the free end of the rope, he found himself caught by the blustering wind and swung back and forth like a pendulum; he was alternately buffeted against the rocks or sent see-sawing over the waves thudding underneath. His weight threatened the final stake holding the *estamperche*. Fortunately, before it yielded and sent him to his death, Joyaux and the others heard his yell and slithered down to drag him over the worst of the ascent.

On the cliff-top they had to go warily since Bonaparte's invasion army had their bivouacs everywhere. Splitting up, they marched at fifty-yard intervals keeping to the fields and woods. Beyond the Dieppe road, they found their first refuge, Pageot's farm at Guilmecourt where the farmer's wife prepared stew, homemade cheese and bread then led them to the barn.

For Cadoudal, sleep came slowly that night. France meant too many things, stirred too many emotions. This was Normandy where his friend, General Louis de Frotté had kept several republican divisions pegged with a few hundred Chouans. Poor Frotté had agreed to the so-called pacification and Bonaparte's amnesty. He'd got his pacification — against a firing-squad wall with his lieutenants. Bonaparte's Florentine justice!

Lying looking at the stars through the open eaves of the barn, Cadoudal wondered if they could change the course of history with just this one blow. A single thought filled his mind: this time he would neither cede nor run; this time he would leave his bones in France whatever happened.

On the following night they marched for the second relay post, the Poterie farm on the edge of Eue Forest. There, Jacques Detrimont, a royalist for his sixty-eight years, fed, lodged and fêted them. From there, they turned south, sleeping during daylight and trekking through the darkness for another six relay posts between the Poterie and Paris.

Eighteen months before, Cadoudal had delegated one of his most brilliant and trusted lieutenants, Charles d'Hozier, to return to Paris and establish this Liberty Line. He and one of the Caillard brothers, Raoul, had done the job to perfection, finding inns, farms, convents where royalists sympathies ran strong and no one questioned a mammoth figure and six men who slept with their heads on knapsacks which hid a brace of pistols and at least one dagger.

Two days march from Paris, Raoul Gaillard came to greet them and explained how Hozier intended to smuggle the seven of them into the capital.

6

When he arrived with three men and a handgrip at the meeting-point beyond the Saint-Denis Gate on the morning of 30 August, Charles d'Hozier looked and acted as though he were playing an elaborate game. Yet, he had spared nothing to ensure his general got past the gendarmes and troops on this important post. His eighteen months in the capital he had used to good purpose, setting up as a coach-hirer near the Temple Prison under the name of Aulnay.

Among his many republican clients, no one ever guessed this handsome, soft-spoken, jokey young man had once acted as page to the executed Louis XVI and knew Versailles, the Tuileries and the Château Saint-Cloud like his own lodgings; no one suspected he was now a central figure in a conspiracy to capture or murder Bonaparte, the First Consul, and destroy the republic. Hozier had chosen his business to allow him to supply transport and horses to take Bonaparte to the coast and exile.

With him had come Colonel Louis-Charles de Sol, one of Cadoudal's commanders who had been operating underground in Paris for months, and two strangers; one of these men, built massively like Cadoudal, disappeared and Hozier whispered they had brought him to fool the guards; Cadoudal would don the same clothing as the decoy and they had papers under his name, Monsieur Larive.

Cadoudal met the fourth man, Hyacinthe Bouvet de Lozier, who had helped set up the relay stations and establish hiding-places and contacts in Paris; he had also found them a mansion for the princes when they arrived to lead the coup.

Cadoudal shook hands, then wondered why Bouvet's seemed so limp and damp; he did not care much for men with spaniel eyes and droopy mouths and the bitter turn of phrase which Bouvet seemed to affect. Yet, Charles had guaranteed him, and he seemed to have the king's interests at heart.

That afternoon, the republican guards hardly gave them a second glance as they passed through the gate with their friend, Aulnay (Hozier). By evening, Cadoudal and his companions, Aimé Joyaux and Louis de Sol, had settled into their first cache with the Denant family at their tavern, La Cloche d'Or in Rue du Bac.

There, with maps, they went over the Liberty Line, marking each farm, inn, convent and church and committing these to memory before burning the map. Only a handful of men knew the Liberty Line, but they would have to use it thirty or forty times to bring in the 300 or 400 men who would form the core of the *coup d'état*.

Charles d'Hozier had done them proud. They had two rooms in Père Denant's tavern giving on the main thoroughfare of the royalist Saint-Germain district. They also had a cache made by a master hand. Hozier had somehow discovered a little cabinet-maker called Spain with no political sympathies but a craftsman's pride and a long thirst for red wine that needed satisfying.

In just over a year, Spain had made a dozen hideouts in houses rented under assumed names by Hozier and his royalist friends. For Cadoudal and his two aides he had built false walls so cunningly no one suspected they concealed an alcove where three men could sit or lie comfortably. They had an escape trap leading to another alcove under the stairs and another trap at the back of the tavern. Both entrance doors swivelled vertically at the touch of a hidden latch known only to the three men and Père Denant.

La Cloche d'Or had become the Paris headquarters of the Chouans and royalists. To the casual observer, it looked like a normal tavern — a bit sordid, full of coachmen, peasants, horse-traders, *petit bourgeois* and a smattering of soldiers to lend it tone and keep prying gendarmes at bay. Underneath those disguises, dozens of noblemen had returned secretly to Paris and picked up their orders and messages through the network Hozier and Cadoudal had established. Cadoudal had several disguises, clothing bought by Hozier's friends over months from Le Petit Saint-Thomas store which allowed him to masquerade as anything from a street cleaner to a lawyer.

Like his co-conspirators, Cadoudal moved only at night. Although he had a long list of Bourbon supporters, he met only a handful of them, men he could trust absolutely. Let Bonaparte learn even of his presence in Paris and his mission would fail. Yet, through a dozen or so contacts he soon constructed an intricate network of monarchist cells to which he could smuggle arms and munitions and relay orders for the *coup d'état*.

He soon saw Bonaparte had lost all royalist support by his curt refusal to negotiate with Louis XVIII; he learned, too, the First Consul had earned the wrath of even moderate republicans by signing his Concordat with the Pope. This republican unrest centred around General Jean-Victor Moreau who, with his wife, hated Bonaparte and Joséphine.

If Pichegru could persuade his old second-in-command to join them, they could also recruit generals like Macdonald, Lecourbe and half-a-dozen others. In the senate, the influential Abbé Emmanuel-Joseph Sieyès had mustered more than thirty members ready to denounce Bonaparte as a dictator, if he was given military backing. And waiting in the wings, men like Fouché and Talleyrand would not hesitate to destroy Bonaparte if this served their interests.

With great caution, they assembled stocks of weapons, musket and pistol balls and powder, stolen from republican arsenals or smuggled in from Brittany. Cadoudal had dispatched Saint-Hilaire and Brèche to the west to funnel arms to the capital and alert Chouan units that would attack republican garrisons during the *coup d'état*.

At the same time, royalist supporters in the republican army procured uniforms which would serve to confuse government troops on the night; even among the consular guard billeted in the Tuileries, they had half-a-dozen men planted, and soon had collected enough guardsmen's uniforms for thirty men, half the strength of Bonaparte's personal escort. But, almost as though they had wind of something, Bonaparte and his favorite lackey, General René Savary began to change the officers and men of the guard from time to time.

Pichegru was right in saying the First Consul never failed to exploit the surprise element. Night after night for weeks, Cadoudal, Joyaux, Louis de Sol and Coster-Saint-Victor patrolled the route between the Tuileries and Bonaparte's two residences just west of the capital — Malmaison, the country mansion chosen by Joséphine, and the Château of Saint-Cloud, an imposing palace which had housed so many French monarchs. Between the Paris ramparts and those two estates lay several miles of open country in which fifty determined men might ambush and annihilate the First Consul's small escort.

Yet, never once did the man use the same route at the same hour. And he did likewise for official engagements announced in *Le Moniteur*, changing times and routes at the last moment. Nor could his staff at the Tuileries, Saint-Cloud or Malmaison predict where he might be or what he might do at any hour of the day or night. His chef had been known to roast as many as thirty chickens to have a fresh one ready for him while Joséphine and her guests waited for him to arrive from they knew not where. Because of Bonaparte's will-o'-the-wisp tactics, Cadoudal decided to double his attacking force and choose eight ambush points in the woods between Paris and the two residences. Dozens of times he, Joyaux and Hozier observed, watches in hand, the cavalcade of fifty consular guards escorting the berlin transporting Bonaparte, Joséphine and her daughter Hortense.

Spectating on this scene, Cadoudal reflected that the little Corsican general had come a long way since their meeting just over three years before in the Minerva Salon of the Tuileries. Even the recollection of that stormy hour made his blood run hot.

He had gone with Guillaume Hyde de Neuville and other royalist leaders to discuss peace terms. Speaking to the nobles, Bonaparte had ointment on his tongue, but with him, Cadoudal, son of a Breton yeoman, a commoner, a guerrilla leader, the First Consul had strutted around like a king — or an emperor. He had offered him a regiment in his republican army! And when he had rejected that sop, threatened to march ten divisions into Brittany to snuff out resistance.

What right had this jerky little man in a shabby, stained, colonel's uniform to dictate his terms to him, or anybody else? They had bawled at each other like two fishwives. During that row, he noticed General Rapp had left the door open and two guards stood there, pistols cocked, accompanied by Bourrienne, the Consul's secretary. He had emerged from the Tuileries sweating with fury, his big hands twitching involuntarily.

'I don't know why I didn't pick up that little man and squeeze the life out of him with these hands,' he said to Hyde de Neuville. When the aristocrat murmured something in Bonaparte's defence, Cadoudal brushed it aside. 'No, the little tyrant has changed his tune since so many people have licked his boots and so many priests have bowed the knee. Pacification. Amnesty. All sham! He'll soon have us all behind bars.' And they had fled to England to lie low.

This time he would leave nothing to chance. His reconnaissance done, he chose Malmaison as his most probable attack point, siting and reconnoitring five places around its entrance; he picked another three on the Saint-Cloud route, one alongside the track through the Champs Elysées, on a patch of overgrown waste ground. All his ambush areas had easy access to the Liberty Line. This time he would not rest until Bonaparte was on the way to the coast — or dead.

7

Although he did not take to Bouvet de Lozier, the man turned out to have his uses. His spaniel face and languid manner appealed to ladies, especially an aristocratic beauty called Madame Costard de Saint-Leger, whose husband had perished on the guillotine and who hated her new rulers enough to risk the same fate. At Bouvet's suggestion, she rented a mansion beyond the Champs Elysées at Chaillot; it sat in its own grounds with a gate fronting on the Versailles road. Trees hid the main building and camouflaged the alleys leading to the Seine on the other side.

Apart from its charm and luxury, the country mansion had one other advantage: from its cellars ran an underground network of passages traversing the old Chaillot quarries and surfacing 400 metres away at Sainte-Perrine.

No one could have designed a better sanctuary for the Comte d'Artois and the Duc de Berri when they arrived to take over the Government of France in the name of Louis XVIII.

Marie de Saint-Leger had given her staff instructions to treat her friends like family members. So, Cadoudal, Joyaux, Louis de Sol, Hozier, Bouvet and others used the mansion as a second headquarters: for himself and his officers, Cadoudal insisted on impeccable dress and manners so that servants and caretakers would suspect nothing.

Cadoudal dressed as elegantly as the new nobility gyrating round the Tuileries, donning satin breeches, buckled shoes, ruffed shirt, silk cravat and fashionable frock coat — all found by Hozier.

In England, he had perfected various disguises, fooling even close friends. He also enjoyed playing cat and mouse with the police or the army. Five long years he had lain low in Brittany while the Directory, then Bonaparte had tried to track and flush him out. Dozens of Fouché's spies who attempted to shoot or poison him finished before Chouan firing squads.

Marie de Saint-Leger showed him round the house herself. Somehow, during the Revolution, it had preserved its Louis Quatorze tables, chairs, writing bureau, and four-poster beds, the sort of trappings Artois would find familiar and which had mostly gone to feed fires and warm *sans-culotte* hands. Chequered marble floors and gilded wainscoting set off the period furniture.

Not immune to beauty in women, Cadoudal thought Marie de Saint-Leger just as impressive as her discreet pavilion. She had a slender, lissom figure and flaunted her breasts and hips by wearing close-fitting gowns and embroidered bodices; blonde curls like frothy bubbles covered her head, framing her oval face.

But what impressed Cadoudal most was her spirit that shrugged aside the grave danger of letting her mansion to men who were determined to overthrow the republican government. A fatalist, she had spent months in the Carmes Prison, just escaping the guillotine; she amused Cadoudal with first-hand stories of General Lazare Hoche and Joséphine de Beauharnais (now Madame Bonaparte) who had fallen in love and shared a cell while waiting for Robespierre to mark them both for the guillotine. Bonaparte knew nothing of that love affair, though he had heard of the many others she had carried on while he was campaigning in Egypt.

Marie de Saint-Leger demonstrated how parts of the marble floor and gilded wainscoting slid down or back to reveal secret passages along which several hundred aristocrats had made their way to freedom.

Upstairs, she showed him the six bedrooms on two floors. In the master bedroom, which had a downhill view to the Seine, she paused and looked at him, an arch curve on her full, red lips and a crinkling smile round her blue eyes. 'You may use this for yourself, *mon général*,' she murmured.

'But it is for Monsieur le Prince,' Cadoudal cried, as though she were guilty of sacrilege or *lèse-majesté*.

'Would he know if we changed the linen?' she asked, with studied ambiguity. 'After all, I slept here for months — and others, too.'

'Well, I shall sleep downstairs on a camp-bed.'

'A single bed!' Marie de Saint-Leger exclaimed. 'Don't you have anyone to keep you company?'

'No, *madame*.'

'No *petite amie*?'

'If you have to know, I am betrothed to a young lady in the west country.'

'Then fetch her here. I don't mind.'

'*Madame*, neither she nor I would dream of it. We have agreed to marry only when Louis XVIII has been restored to his throne and can bless our marriage himself.'

'But that might be years.'

'Then we shall do what we have done for nearly ten years — wait.'

92

'Oh!' Marie de Saint-Leger realized that with men like General Georges Cadoudal the badinage ended there — although she failed to understand why anyone who was living under the threat of sudden death, either in battle or on the guillotine, did not gather a few rosebuds on the way. Parading her mischievous eyes over Cadoudal's massive figure, appraising his rugged but handsome face and russet curls, she could not help lamenting such a loss to herself, to womanhood in general — and all for some anonymous virgin in an outlandish western province.

For Cadoudal's part, while he admired this lovely young aristocrat, he distrusted the presence of any woman in the operation; he also feared where Bouvet de Lozier's philandering might lead them, for he had several mistresses besides Marie de Saint-Leger and it needed no more than a streak of jealousy or a loose word to betray them all.

As a battlefield general, he had realized war and women did not mix. He had even issued a decree to his own command stating that those men who married under forty years of age would be shot with the civilian officers who had married them; their parents had their property confiscated or paid heavy fines. In his eyes, married men fought with only half their hearts and sexual incontinence weakened the sword arm.

Now they had a house for the princes and bases inside and outside Paris. From the Chaillot house, Cadoudal kept in touch with Saint-Hilaire; he could now pass orders for the Chouans in Brittany and La Vendée, and for the Caillard brothers, Raoul and Armand, who were running the Liberty Line. They were escorting handfuls of men, trained by Guillemot in Winchester, and finding them hideouts in the capital.

Within a month, they had just over fifty men concealed in the Saint-Germain and Marais districts and at least a dozen caches of arms and ammunition. Charles d'Hozier and Bouvet had the job of setting up these arsenals in Paris and its outlying suburbs; they had ingenious schemes for smuggling and hiding these weapons in various royalist houses. Hozier took the biggest risk, for much of the contraband transited through his coach-hiring sheds and his lodgings.

Six weeks after Cadoudal's arrival, Hozier and Bouvet appeared in the Rue de Bac. Hozier was disguised as a mason, in overalls, floppy bonnet and baggy trousers; Bouvet was wearing a black, claw-hammer coat, breeches and cocked hat which looked like the uniform issued to some of Bonaparte's detectives; he sported side-whiskers which he must have gummed on, though they had not altered his saturnine features.

Hozier came to the point. 'They're searching my house and stables,' he said. 'Somebody tipped off the police I'd cached two hundred pounds of gunpowder in the house.'

'And have you?'

Hozier nodded. 'A friend of mine in the police whispered they were going to search my premises. I just had time to plank the powder behind the chimney in a cache made by Spain.' Hozier had masons working upstairs; he had borrowed clothes from one and walked past the police as they entered to arrest him and make the search.

'If they find that powder and trace where it came from we're finished,' Cadoudal grunted. He ordered Bouvet to meet them at Hozier's premises in Rue Vieille-la-Temple with a two-in-hand cab, which he, Cadoudal, would drive. He quickly donned a coachman's uniform — one of his disguises — consisting of a coat with a cape, riding boots and beaver hat. Hozier found a hired cab to take them to the stables in the Marais district. From the opposite side of the street, they watched the police guard on the gate until two detectives emerged muttering insults about informants who gave false information.

As soon as the police had disappeared, the two men entered Hozier's house, which formed the back of the yard where he guarded his coaches and horses during the day. His two loaded pistols ready, Cadoudal kept an eye on the door while Hozier removed a brick from the vast, open chimney and exerted a slight pressure, which caused the side of the chimney to swing back. Spain had excelled himself; constructing a wooden framework blocked in with masonry. Behind this contraption lay a dozen small barrels of gunpowder — enough to blow up the whole street.

Bouvet arrived with a carriage, hired on the other side of Paris. At dusk, the three men loaded the gunpowder into the vehicle and set out for a safe hideout in the Saint-Martin district.

As they passed the local police prefecture, a gendarme spotted Hozier and blew his whistle, alerting a police cab, which sat there with two gendarmes in it. Within a moment it was giving chase, and a mounted policeman was clattering behind it.

Now in the driver's seat, Cadoudal whipped the two horses into a gallop and rattled through the cobbled streets, scattering pedestrians and spreading panic among the coach horses he passed and evaded.

'Throw the lanterns at them, Charles,' he shouted.

Hozier pulled the two glass lanterns from their sockets and hurled them behind the coach where they burst into flames and set glass splinters flying. For a few moments, it slowed the pursuit but, more important, made them difficult to locate in the dark.

With the mounted policeman gaining on them, Cadoudal made for the Canal Saint-Martin. 'I'm going to dump the stuff there,' he called to Hozier.

'No, Georges, they'll find it.'

Hozier, who knew Paris brick by brick, suddenly seized the reins and jerked the horses round on themselves and steered them into a narrow street. 'First left, left again and then right,' he ordered Cadoudal, who obeyed his directions. It took another half-dozen twists and turns through tight streets before they were sure they had shaken off the police.

They still had to cache the gunpowder, but Hozier knew a safe house in La Vilette where they hid it in a small shed.

During the chase, Bouvet had said and done nothing, but had sat in the back of the cab on top of the powder. As he dismounted, Cadoudal noticed he was trembling and clutching a box of phosphor matches in one hand and holding a couple of inches of fuse in the other.

'What were you going to do with those things?' Cadoudal asked.

'Blow myself into the next world,' Bouvet said, with no humor in his white, frightened face.

'And us with you!' Cadoudal exclaimed. 'You mean you'd have sacrificed the whole undertaking?'

Bouvet nodded.

'But why?' Hozier demanded.

Bouvet did not answer.

'Why?' Cadoudal insisted.

Bouvet hesitated. 'I don't intend to spend the rest of my life in prison,' he muttered.

Both his companions stared at him, but said nothing. However, from that moment and that incident, Cadoudal wondered about Bouvet. How deep did his dedication to the king go? How would he stand up under real strain? Still, they needed him for his influential friends, his knowledge of the workings of government and the contacts essential for the success of their *coup d'état*. All the same, he would have preferred someone without a wet handshake, muddy eyes, a lugubrious face and such a selfish regard for his own skin.

8

Eleven o'clock was tolling from Saint-Roch Church when Cadoudal and his companions sighted the consular coach with its green and yellow emblem as it passed between the guards' barracks and the Tuileries. Allowing it a start of a hundred yards, their own two-in-hand followed its bobbing lanterns along the Quai des Tuileries and round the bend of the River Seine at the Place de la Concorde. Louis le Ridant was driving their coach with Cadoudal, Joyaux and Louis de Sol inside, wrapped to the eyes in heavy coats against the chill October night and inquisitive policemen.

At the Allée des Veuves, beyond the deserted expanse of the Champs Elysées, the First Consul's coach bore right and trotted down a tree-lined avenue of aristocratic mansions to stop before a small pavilion.

Le Ridant halted at a mansion further back, though keeping the first coach in view. In the lantern light, the four conspirators observed Bonaparte's slight figure descend then gesture to his three companions as he disappeared into the house with his brisk, splay-footed walk.

Le Ridant saw his three passengers vanish into the bushes before turning his horses round and making for the river.

'Aimé, can you see who they are?' Cadoudal whispered.

'Murat's one of them,' Joyaux replied. 'I'd know that squashed nose and gypsy face anywhere. Savary's one of the other two, but I can't place the third man.'

Another thing identified General Joachim Murat, the brother-in-law whom Bonaparte had recently appointed Governor of Paris; he glittered like a goldsmith's shop front with the amount of braid he wore. He looked like a bullfighter, Cadoudal thought. Beside him, General René Savary stood a full head shorter, a shapeless silhouette in cape, shako and thigh boots. Now chief of the consular gendarmerie, Savary had once served under Pichegru and Moreau. But they could expect no help from that flint-eyed and black-hearted villain who had sold himself, body and soul, to Bonaparte.

'I think the third man's just a captain of the consular guard,' Louis de Sol said, crawling back from the edge of the garden.

'How many men do you reckon they've posted round the place?'

'I'd say about fifty gendarmes and maybe twenty policemen,' de Sol answered.

Talk and laughter reached them from the ground-floor room of the small mansion. Half an hour later, a lamp or lustre illuminated an upstairs room briefly then darkness and silence fell on the building.

'If we gave old Duchâtel a brace of pistols and turned him loose in his own bedroom he'd do the job for us,' Aimé Joyaux murmured.

'It's not the way,' Cadoudal replied. He felt like some thief or voyeur, tailing Bonaparte and spying on his latest mistress, but he had stifled his scruples with the thought it might make kidnapping the tyrant that much easier.

Their informants had told them about Bonaparte's affair with Madame Duchâtel, the 20-year-old wife of a complacent state councillor thrice her age and with only a tenth of her sexual energy. Bonaparte even flaunted the willowy, blonde girl in front of Joséphine at Saint-Cloud, and rumour said she had surprised them in the act of love. She had raged at Bonaparte and ordered his valet, Constant, to rent the house in the Allée des Veuves so that he and his paramour would not meet under her roof. So, twice a week, the berlin left the Tuileries for this hidden mansion. But, as always with the First

101

Consul, no one could ever forecast the day or hour.

In the weeks that they had followed his coach, the plotters noticed one thing: now Murat or another of Bonaparte's trusted generals accompanied him and kept vigil until the First Consul took leave of his mistress. And since neither Bonaparte nor his friends feared enraged husbands, the Chouans assumed the guard was protecting him against possible assassination attempts.

His general staff had good reason to stay close to their master; Bonaparte's amorous impulses took him into some curious corners of Paris, the twisting back alleys of the Marais, the central boulevards and the old dwellings in the Île de la Cité.

Cadoudal had tailed him to Auteuil where he dallied with Madame de Vaudey, one of Joséphine's palace companions, until she made too many demands on him; he made secret visits to Laure Junot, wife of one of his generals, in a house near Malmaison; for some time, he had taken as his mistress the great Italian opera singer, Giuseppina Grassini and would either meet her in her hotel or at the Tuileries, smuggled in by Constant or Roustam, the Mameluke servant he had brought back with him from his Egyptian campaign.

But whether by calculation or caprice, Bonaparte never made trysts with these ladies. Someone from his staff came to announce his arrival an hour or two in advance, which gave no one time to prepare an attempt on his life.

Cadoudal wondered what these women, or women in general, meant to a man like Bonaparte. Did they flatter his self-esteem or vanity? Or did he consider them as so many conquests? Like the countries he had raped in the name of liberty, did he seduce these women in the name of love that he felt only for himself?

For two hours, the Chouan leaders lay in the bushes not more than thirty yards from Murat and Savary. Finally Bonaparte emerged, quick-striding down the driveway, drawing a cape around his shoulders.

'It would be easy, General,' Aimé Joyaux whispered, but Cadoudal gripped his pistol arm to signify, No. He had pledged his word to the princes, to Pichegru, to everyone concerned in the *coup d'état*. Anyway, if they killed Bonaparte and two of his generals that would not alter the pattern of government or society in France one jot.

Despite himself, Cadoudal had to respect some sides of Bonaparte's character. He had shadowed him as he walked, unarmed, through Paris with only an aide for company when everyone knew he had narrowly escaped more than a dozen assassination attempts.

No one could deny his popularity. Whether on foot or riding his white Arab through the streets, he gathered crowds who surged round to applaud or just touch him. He knew how to win people over and make them his disciples, as Pichegru had said. He braved and seemed even to taunt death, compelling his officers and men to follow his example. And those who had faced death together and witnessed others die around them shared a camaraderie like no other. Cadoudal, the soldier, understood the truth of that.

In just over two months, Cadoudal had men planted near every house Bonaparte visited to meet his various mistresses; his spies in the Tuileries, Saint-Cloud and Malmaison reported on the First Consul's movements and the comings and goings of his ministers and generals. Not once did any of these informants mention that Bonaparte or his police suspected a band of royalist conspirators was operating in the capital; not once did anyone hint that Bonaparte feared a plot against his life let alone a *coup d'état* to oust him.

Cadoudal felt so certain his plan was

foolproof and his men had carried out every one of his injunctions about security that he could not believe it when two blows fell in quick succession during October.

★　★　★

He had ordered Jean-Pierre Querelle to quit his hideout in Rue Rochechouart, go to Brittany and bring back information about the mobilization of the Chouans. But fearing arrest for debts if he showed face in his native Sarzeau, the man had disobeyed; instead of making the trip, he had written letters to his brother-in-law, an apothecary in Vannes, asking about the morale in Brittany, the influence of the priests and the quantity of arms reaching the province from England. One letter found its way, through the apothecary's mistress, to the police; others opened by the Paris police led them to Querelle who now faced charges of sedition.

When Cadoudal learned from one of his men that Querelle had been arrested and lay in the Temple Prison, he cursed his weakness for overlooking the surgeon's lapse in Hastings. Yet his agents reassured him, saying Querelle had given virtually nothing away. At his captors' behest he had written to Aimé Joyaux, whom they believed was still in

England, to ask for credit so that the police could find out who was financing the Chouans. He had also misled them with harmless information.

More disturbing was the fact that Bonaparte himself seemed to have pressed his chief justice, Claude-Ambroise Régnier to force Querelle to confess he was spying for the royalists in Paris. But Régnier had ignored the First Consul's directive and Querelle had disappeared into the Bicêtre Prison, a forgotten man. But could they rely on him to hold his tongue? Cadoudal wondered if his whole conspiracy would stand or fall around a wizened, pock-marked little sawbones with fluttering eyelids and a palsied hand.

Soon he had other worries. Colonel Louis de Sol burst into their latest hideout in the Saint-Martin district. 'I'm lost,' he whispered. 'They've spotted me on the boulevard.' He had given two policemen the slip and come to warn his companions in case he had been traced to this address. While Cadoudal and Joyaux crawled into their cache behind the false wall of the alcove bed, de Sol sat waiting for the knock on the door; after half an hour, when no one had arrived, he told them he would try to pierce the barriers around Paris and reach Brittany. They both urged him to hide until the *coup d'état* but he felt he might betray their presence in Paris and foil their plot. Next morning, they heard he was lying, chained, in the Temple Prison.

Cadoudal did not worry about de Sol. He would die rather than talk. But what he gleaned about his arrest from the Tuileries gave him more concern. For it seemed Bonaparte himself had got wind of de Sol's movements in Paris and had personally ordered Régnier to lock him up. He remembered what Pichegru had said about Bonaparte — what a brilliant detective he would make. It appeared he was right about that, too.

If the First Consul and his agents had come this close to them, he had better warn Pichegru and the princes to lie low. Through the Gaillard brothers and John Wright he sent word to Pichegru in London while warning everybody in the Paris network to keep their heads down until he knew how deeply Bonaparte had probed.

9

As the weeks went by Cadoudal's confidence returned. They had not discovered the Liberty Line, nor the landing site on the cliffs at Biville. Five times, Cadoudal himself, rode or trekked along the chain of inns, farms and convents accompanied by the Gaillard brothers; with each run another dozen of Guillemot's Chouans filtered into Paris, ready for the strike.

At the beginning of December 1803, Cadoudal went to collect one of the most prominent nobles in Artois' circle — Armand de Polignac. Eldest son of Marie Antoinette's favourite lady-in-waiting, he had pleaded to join the conspiracy with his brother, Jules. Cadoudal could have done without two such quaint aristocrats who viewed the *coup d'état* and the abduction of Bonaparte as an amusing game. Out of deference to Artois he accepted them. Polignac assured him Artois and Berri would arrive with Pichegru in the middle of January 1804.

They had prepared everything for the two princes, who would lead the coup and take over the government once it had been realized. They cleaned the Chaillot mansion and Hozier had his best coach waiting to bring them round the perimeter of the capital with clothing to disguise them. Two guides went to England to guarantee that nothing went wrong between the Kent port of Deal and Biville.

On 16 January, 1804, Cadoudal and a few of his most trusted officers waited at La Poterie farm while Gaston Froche went to fetch the party from the smugglers' cove. One after the other, they arrived, exhausted by their night march. General Charles Pichegru hardly had time to remove his broad-brimmed hat and green, silk-lined cape before Cadoudal demanded, 'Are the princes with you?'

'No.'

'In God's name, why not?'

'They've decided to wait until I have made contact with General Moreau. The moment that is done they will come.'

'But everything is ready for them.'

'They want to make sure we've co-ordinated the kidnapping with the *coup d'état* and the royalists and republicans will move together. Moreau's the key to all that.'

'And if he doesn't agree to march with us?'

Pichegru hesitated, then shrugged. 'We'll have to find someone else who will.'

'That means we're lost,' Cadoudal cried. 'Artois won't set foot in France if Moreau says no.'

Pichegru shook his head, nodding towards young Jules de Polignac who had just entered the farmhouse. Many courtiers thought him Artois' bastard son. 'Monsieur le Prince wouldn't have allowed him and his brother to become involved in this hazardous business if he didn't mean to lead the royalist movement himself. And I have also brought the Marquis de Rivière.'

Cadoudal had to acknowledge the older general's logic. Artois had sent his most trusted friend and adviser, the Marquis de Rivière, to look after his interests and decide when they should make their appearance.

A week later they entered Paris separately; no one bothered the well-dressed gentleman from Rouen, on a business trip; no one suspected that on the previous occasion when he had passed the Saint-Denis Gate, sixteen gendarmes escorted his barred cage to the coast then embarked him for the penal settlement of Devil's Island.

★　★　★

A week after settling into the mansion at Chaillot, the former republican general and

Cadoudal drove in separate cabs to the Boulevard de la Madeleine in the centre of Paris; a coach stood in the shadows of an alley near the Rue des Capucines. A figure descended and approached them.

'Pichegru!'

'Moreau, *mon vieux*.'

Both generals embraced each other. While their bodyguards kept watch, they took their places in Moreau's coach, followed by Cadoudal.

'They tell me you've come to rid us of Bonaparte,' Moreau said.

'They tell me you'd like to get rid of him almost as much as he'd like to get rid of you,' Pichegru retorted.

He explained that even in London they knew how Bonaparte detested Moreau for his battlefield successes, especially Hohenlinden, and for the Moreau Club where disaffected and restive republicans, officers and senators, foregathered in the general's house to discuss ways of curing the country of the Corsican Disease.

'Our only problem is how,' Moreau said.

Pichegru turned to Cadoudal, concealed in a corner of the coach. 'You've heard of General Georges Cadoudal, or Gideon,' he said. 'He's a Breton like yourself and he's the one man who can topple Bonaparte.'

Moreau and Cadoudal shook hands, then the Chouan whispered the outline of his scheme to abduct Bonaparte and hand him over to the English who would exile him on an island in the middle of the South Atlantic. Moreau listened in silence until Cadoudal had finished, then murmured, 'So, you need somebody to take Bonaparte's place.'

'What do you mean?' Cadoudal cried. 'You must know we already have that somebody — the lawful ruler of France.'

Moreau laughed. 'If you mean the Bourbons, this country wouldn't have them back at any price after the way they behaved and the chaos they caused.'

'Then who did you think I was acting for?' Cadoudal snapped.

'I didn't know,' Moreau replied. 'But if Bonaparte goes there's only one man can take his place.'

'You mean — you!' Cadoudal spluttered, and could hardly speak for choking back his wrath. 'Do you think I came here to change one republican general for another?'

'Nobody's stupid enough to think the Bourbons can take over immediately. Not even themselves.'

'All right,' Cadoudal said, 'if you think you can govern the country better than

Bonaparte, you go ahead and get rid of him on your own.'

'Alas, I have neither the men nor the means.'

'Then you have to accept my terms — the Bourbon princes or nothing.'

'Just try getting the people to accept them. They won't — not without an interim government and a plebiscite which would have to be prepared.'

Cadoudal turned to Pichegru. 'What do you think, General?'

'Moreau knows the capital and the mood of the people better than both of us, and he has lots of friends in the representative body and the senate. He's probably right.'

Moreau seized on this opening. If Bonaparte went, he, Moreau, would become First Consul provisionally with Pichegru Second Consul; as far as the royalists went, they would obtain a complete amnesty, the restoration of their property and would be free to come and go; he ruled out a Third Consul, representing the monarchy, even Cadoudal, since no one in France outside the western provinces would accept a Chouan general.

'So, what do we get out of it?' Cadoudal cried, forgetting in his fury they were plotting kidnapping, murder and sedition in the heart of Paris. 'We have the honour of serving under General Moreau instead of General Bonaparte. If that's the way you look at it, then carry out the *coup d'état* without our help.'

At that, he dismounted and returned to his own carriage where Joyaux and Bouvet de Lozier were waiting. 'Moreau wants us to kill or kidnap Bonaparte so that he can step into his shoes,' he growled. 'Man for man, I prefer the one that's there now to this jumped-up general.'

'He's betrayed us,' Bouvet muttered through his teeth. 'He got us all here believing he was for us, and now he's not prepared to do anything.'

'Well, let him get on with it,' Cadoudal said as they left.

It took a week and all of Pichegru's eloquence to win Cadoudal round. Despite his misgivings, even he realized that without Moreau they could accomplish nothing; the princes would desist and the vital strike and *coup d'état* would founder. It did seem that all republican resistance to Bonaparte revolved round the young, handsome general who rivalled the First Consul's military genius in the popular mind.

And Moreau's wife, something of a firebrand had recruited high-ranking officers, politicians and influential bourgeois to her husband's cause, for she hated the new caesar and the court he was creating around himself and her personal enemy, Joséphine. Pichegru revealed that already more than thirty senators had secretly expressed their intention of voting Bonaparte out of office and replacing him with Moreau if someone took care of the soldiers.

Reluctantly, Cadoudal let Pichegru solder over the differences between them and Moreau and finally they reached a compromise: they would carry out the abduction and *coup d'état* and all three would assume command and give the people time to choose whether or not they wished the return of the Bourbons.

Cadoudal counted on the appearance of the princes to convince Frenchmen they had only one alternative to the deposed Bonaparte. So, while Pichegru and Moreau were discussing strategy, he put in hand final preparations for the abduction of the First Consul.

Between the Tuileries and Bonaparte's other two residences, he chose the streets where he would place his most trusted Chouans under Hozier, Coster, Bouvet, Joyaux and others. He picked the bridges they would barricade and control during and after their attack on the consular guard, and also those they would mine and destroy. His men in ambush, dressed like consular guards, would seize Bonaparte's senior officers while others would have arrested or killed Murat, Savary, Junot, Rapp and other generals.

William Pitt's gold would play its part now: detachments would ride through the capital scattering handfuls of gold and silver, crying. '*Vive le roi!*' Special Chouan squads would set public buildings ablaze and let off charges of gunpowder at strategic points throughout Paris to convince people the royalists had landed in strength. Uprisings in the west would reinforce this idea.

Meanwhile, Pichegru and Moreau with as many of their old comrades as they could muster would appear in the senate to demand that body's sanction for the new government; at this moment, Joyaux, the Gaillard brothers and a handful of Cadoudal's best officers would be taking turns to smuggle Bonaparte, dead or alive, to the coast and an English man-o'-war. For himself Cadoudal would stay in Paris to rally the royalists and ensure a triumphal welcome for Artois when he arrived. He did not intend to allow Moreau to steal power, which their coup had placed in his hands.

He had only two things to settle before

alerting the princes in London that it merely needed their presence in Paris to carry out the strike against Bonaparte. Now, he had more than 200 of his best Chouans in the capital and could count on the support of several hundred determined royalists, he wanted with him the rest of Guillemot's men from Winchester with their leader. Secondly, he must make a last trip to Brittany to ensure Saint-Hilaire and his other lieutenants there had organized the combined assault on towns to divert reinforcements from Paris. Bonaparte had gone to Boulogne to inspect the army and fleet of barges which would invade England, and would be absent for at least three days. So Cadoudal decided to take the opportunity to revisit his home ground and meet his men and their leaders.

He also wanted to see his sweetheart, Lucrèce Mercier.

10

After three interminable years he had come home. Like some aged gundog, he felt he was rediscovering old haunts through his five senses. Nothing, it seemed, ever changed his part of Lower Brittany. Its stone cromlechs stood as they had from time immemorial on the road he had trodden as a boy from his family homestead at Kerléano and the village school at Auray, and with them, druid piles and cairns and calvaries in this land where superstition and paganism had merged into Christian belief. Several fresh wolf paws nailed to barn doors proved how wild the countryside remained and how hard superstition died.

His Brittany had a perfume all of its own; in the air hung the tang of salt and seaweed meeting the earthy smell of turnips and stored apples, just as the plough and the dinghy, the sandpiper and the lark kept company in this region where sea and land and sky fused and the islands floated on the shimmering ocean. Cadoudal could never tire of gazing at the patchwork of colours, the grey rocks clashing with purple heather and black oaks contrasting with the dazzling white of the Lanveau marshes.

He had not forgotten the heady smell of mussels stewing on the hob, or the taste of pancakes and bannocks; his ear and tongue became attuned to Armorican speech with its burring accent; his eye dwelt on the women toiling in the fields or on farms in their traditional black dresses and white coifs. Like their men they, too, only spoke when they had something to say. Unlike Parisians with their formal politeness which meant nothing, and their nasal gab which meant even less.

No, nothing altered Brittany. Not even pacification which had left the province and neighbouring La Vendée with a population of 200,000 out of an original half a million: 300,000 of his folk had found peace — republican peace. Eternal peace. Yet, his ancestors had fought Julius Caesar and his Roman legions in the way he was tussling with this modern caesar.

For him it had all begun not long after he had quit Saint-Yves College in Vannes when he and two comrades had witnessed four republican soldiers raping a local girl. He had seized one of their swords and killed two of the men before asking himself why. His friends had accounted for the others. Since then, he had flitted from one secret hideout

119

to another; even when he became the king's general he could halt only long enough to kill a few more republicans and plan his next battle.

They had pillaged his home and gaoled his mother, who had died in Brest Prison hospital bearing her tenth child; they had killed his brother, Julian, on Bonaparte's orders; they had murdered his best friend, Pierre Mercier, brother of his sweetheart, Lucrèce. These were just a few of the scores he had to settle with Bonaparte.

On Kerléano, his own home, he could only look from a distance, for Bonaparte's spies kept it under surveillance twenty-four hours a day; he met his aged father and one of his sisters after dark at a friend's house, and they urged him to flee to England and wait until Bonaparte had lost several battles and his hold on the country before returning. Why go on fighting for princes who did nothing for themselves? He could tell them nothing of the plot, merely embrace them and wish them God speed.

Wherever he went, they fêted him like a conqueror, drinking toasts with him in their rough cider and singing their Breton love songs and laments. His old headquarters on île Fortuné remained undiscovered, a measure of Chouan loyalty to him. For two years he had directed his army from this hideout on a promontory of the Etel estuary. Here, he now called a council of war with his senior officers. Saint-Hilaire and Brèche, the artilleryman, assured him that an army of more than 20,000 royalists would attack local garrisons on his signal; Guillemot had infiltrated some of his Winchester band into the area to spread the word of Cadoudal's return among the Chouans. For his part, he confirmed Artois and Berri intended to land in France at the right moment. When he had co-ordinated plans with Chouan leaders, he took leave of them to return to Paris.

Yet, he could not return without seeing Lucrèce, even though he had misgivings about such a meeting. Not only did it entail personal risk but it could jeopardize the whole operation if he were caught. He was aware, too, that such a tryst would place great emotional as well as nervous strain on both of them. Lucrèce and he loved each other, but could not dream of breaking their oath and consummating their love. Yet, regardless of the frustration, he had to see her, just to touch her.

But he also had to weigh carefully a plan for her safety. As the sister of Pierre Mercier — General Mercier La Vendée as they had called him — she must have Bonaparte's spies around her house day and night; he could not see her under her father's roof in their inn, Le Lion d'Or at Château-Gontier; he therefore sent Aimé Joyaux with a message, suggesting she might make an excuse to visit her aunt at Vitré, the first Breton city on the Paris road.

Cadoudal, himself, had to move with infinite caution, journeying from the coast at night in short marches and taking three days to cross the province. Joyaux had found him lodgings inside the old citadel of Vitré under the feudal castle in Rue d'Ambas, and there he waited for Lucrèce.

Two days later Joyaux conducted her to the lodgings after dark. In the fluid candlelight, Cadoudal and she gazed at each other for minutes without speaking. For more than three years they had been kept apart by Cadoudal's exile and by republican troops and gendarmes who garrisoned that part of Mayenne where Lucrèce lived. Now they seemed shy, almost like strangers. If anything, Cadoudal thought Lucrèce looked more beautiful than even his idealized image of her.

So often, in his lonely years in île Fortuné and in England he had longed for her with such intensity that he had the illusion of seeing and even touching her, but now, as she undid her bonnet and slipped out of her heavy cape, his heart began to hammer and his tongue swell in his mouth, choking back the greetings he had rehearsed for hours.

Given a sabre and a dozen revolutionaries in blue uniforms to fight and he had no fear at all. Yet, this slender creature with her quiet movements, her delicate figure, pale, milky skin and blonde hair tied in a simple chignon turned him to water. As though sensing his confusion, Lucrèce came to kiss him on both cheeks.

'God has answered my prayers, Georges,' she whispered.

'I prayed, too, you would be able to come,' he stuttered.

'They couldn't stop me.' She smiled. 'I had to hide in a wine-cart to get past the guard they had round the Lion d'Or. They strengthened the guard because it was gossiped you were back in Brittany.'

'It's what I wanted them to believe.'

'You're not staying, then. Are you going back to England?'

'No, to Paris.'

'But, *mon amour*, they'll catch you and . . . ' Her eyes widened and she gripped his huge hand, unable to complete the thought. He saw her look grow sad and her eyes veil with tears and knew she was thinking of Pierre, her favourite brother, who had all the talents and who said they'd never catch or kill him; and now, no one knew where he lay in Morbihan. And before Pierre, whom they had both loved, she had lost another brother, killed at the head of his Chouans.

Lucrèce gazed at Cadoudal as though she had never really studied him before, or was now noting something about him that troubled her. He had always taken things seriously: his religion; their love; their pledge; those things, and his lonely struggle for his king and his native Brittany. But now, across his brow, under his reddish, curly hair and in the set of his broad face, she read sadness. And she sensed why he had made that perilous journey from Paris and would have to return there, travelling at night and hiding in corners like some tracked beast. She realized, too, why she had answered his heart-cry to meet him in this grim trysting-place in a strange, walled town lined with republican soldiers.

Did he have a presentiment that this furtive rendezvous might be the last of their years of stolen moments? That feeling overwhelmed her. She felt that no Bourbon king would ever bless their marriage only through God would they ever come together. Yet, if God willed it that way, what could they do but submit their wills to His?

Her voice, so thin and weak in her ears, sounded like some stranger's as she whispered, 'Georges, if anything happened to you, I would not want to go on living.'

'Nothing is going to happen to me,' he said, gripping her shoulders. 'But if it does, promise you will go on living and praying for me.'

'But I do pray for you — every day of my life.'

'Just promise.'

'I promise.'

He kissed her, gently, on the mouth then looked at her, smiling. 'Say nothing to anyone, but in another month we'll be together without fearing either God or man,' he murmured.

'You really believe it?' she said.

He nodded. From a pocket, he drew out a small box in gold filigree lined in red velvet and proffered it; Lucrèce turned this reliquary round in her hand, marvelling at its shape and exquisite workmanship. Then, at his insistence, she opened it. Inside, lay a ring which she held up to the candlelight watching its gold reflect the wavering flame.

'But it's a wedding ring,' she whispered. 'You know we cannot . . . our vows will not let us . . . '

'I know. Not until the king comes into his

own and France has come to her senses.' He took her small face in his hands and looked at her gravely. 'Lucrèce, I have the word of Artois himself that he will be the chief witness at our wedding in Paris.'

'The prince is coming back,' she breathed.

'That's why I'm here.'

'But surely Bonaparte is too strong?'

'No one has really put him to the test in France.'

'Georges, you're not going to do anything dangerous for our sake, are you?'

'For France, for the princes — and then for us.'

They fell silent, their minds going back to that evening at Chateau-Gontier ten years before, when Cadoudal was twenty-three and Lucrèce seventeen. In front of their parents at the inn, with Pierre by their side and a few close comrades around them, both had plighted their troth. They promised to love one another with honour, but to keep their love and faith pure and sacrosanct until Louis XVII had taken his father's place on the French throne. Abbé Lebreton had officiated at this simple rite, blessing the couple in God's eyes and praying that they might soon become man and wife.

That ceremony they had celebrated like a wedding, but a wedding without the ultimate act of physical possession, of fusion of their flesh for which they both yearned. Since then, Louis XVII had died and now they prayed for Louis XVIII to return and free them from their vow of sexual abnegation; since then, they had met half-a-dozen times, always hole-and-corner occasions like this, under threat of capture. Yet, they drew strength and hope even from these contacts. At least they had both survived when so many of those they had loved were dead, sacrificed to the cause.

Lucrèce tried the gold band on the left ring finger — the wrong one — and laughed with delight when it fitted perfectly. 'How long, I wonder?' she sighed.

'Not much longer, my love.' He put his arms around her, feeling the frisson of her flesh through the stiff brocade of her dress; in the candlelight, she seemed to tremble and he saw her eyes mist over and felt her cheeks burn when he kissed her there. 'Not much longer, my love,' he said.

For an hour they sat, holding hands tentatively, like new lovers, speaking little as though afraid to betray their real emotions. Finally, Lucrèce rose. Her aunt might think she had fallen into republican hands, she said. Cadoudal accompanied her to the doorway and watched her climb into Joyaux's hired cab.

When he had mounted the stairs to his room, he threw himself on the single bed with a groan and snuffed the candle in case its guttering flame would efface the after-image of his loved one, seared like some brand on his mind.

11

Cadoudal now switched his Paris hideout every week in case Bonaparte's police might follow one of his chief lieutenants and discover him. Only half-a-dozen people knew his movements, and even they had orders to contact him only in emergencies. So, when Coster-Saint-Victor turned up at the beginning of the last week in January, Cadoudal guessed he had something of great importance to reveal.

'Nobody on your back?' he asked.

'No, *mon général*. I took three cabs in three different directions and walked the last ten minutes.'

Coster, of all people, needed to take such precautions, Cadoudal thought, eyeing the floral silk coat, the canary waistcoat and velvet breeches. Still, who wouldn't have taken him for a fop rather than a conspirator? And who could object to Coster's dandyism when he had fought bravely in Brittany and helped several of Saint-Réjant's band to escape after the Saint-Nicaise attempt?

He showed Coster the half-dozen secret compartments Spain had made in this house in Rue Bichat. 'If anybody gives the alarm, you climb in there,' Cadoudal said, pointing to the ceiling. A wall map operated a latch letting down a staircase from the ceiling and disclosing a false platform three feet deep covering the whole room. Cadoudal had a cache in the corridor giving on to the back door.

'Now, what brings you here?' he asked.

Coster obviously considered his information too intriguing to divulge it at one go; he conjured a silver snuffbox from his yellow waistcoat and took an elaborate pinch of snuff; from a coat pocket, he drew a folded paper and held it in front of Cadoudal; it was a theatre poster proclaiming that *Iphigénie in Taurus* by Euripides was playing at the Théâtre-Français.

'Have you noticed it has been running longer than most plays of its kind?'

'Hmmph! I haven't much time or use for plays and play-actors,' Cadoudal grunted.

'But it's an excellent performance. Why, I've seen it now . . . well, it must be nine times.'

'So you go showing yourself off in public places like theatres,' Cadoudal fumed. 'You have strict orders to lie low until you get the password.'

'Ah, but it was in the line of duty, *mon*

général,' Coster smirked.

'Duty? You mean one of your painted whores.'

'Well, yes and no. I really went to keep an eye on the First Consul.'

'Bonaparte? Why is he interested in this play?'

'Exactly what I asked myself when I saw him there night after night,' Coster murmured. 'I thought it was the sacrificial scene . . . you know, when Agamemnon sacrifices his daughter Iphigénie, to appease the war gods and allow the Greek fleet to sail for Troy. I felt that our own caesar would approve such fatherly conduct in the military interest, but it wasn't that at all.'

'Come to the point, Coster.'

Coster flourished the theatre bill on which he had circled one of the prominent names — Mademoiselle George. 'That's what interested him — Mam'zelle George, toast of the Théâtre-Français.'

'Is she his mistress?'

Coster nodded. 'He's mad about her.'

'And you've discovered where she lives?' Coster nodded again. 'All right, we'll put several men around her house to pick him up if he goes there.'

'We can do better than that,' Coster said. He went on to explain Mlle George's

131

background. She was the daughter of a provincial theatre manager and had come to Paris a year ago, aged fifteen, with the famous actress, Françoise Raucourt, who had heard her play minor parts; now, she had made her name in the Théâtre-Français and among the men who frequented it. Lucien Bonaparte, for instance.

'Bonaparte's young brother!'

Coster grinned. 'Oh, he's well down her list. There's Prince Sapieha and half-a-dozen others with Napoleone Buonaparte at their head. You see, she's blonde, blue-eyed, bedworthy — just what he likes.'

Now, Coster continued, the First Consul smuggles her into the Tuileries or Saint-Cloud three or four times a week. Joséphine could scratch her eyes out except that Mlle George stood half as tall again as Madame Bonaparte and even Caesar had to stand on tiptoe to kiss her. He had even planned to transport the whole theatre to Saint-Cloud to play *Iphigénie* in antique costume, but Joséphine had threatened mayhem. So, the First Consul had taken to visiting her at a rented house.

Cadoudal cut the recital short. 'What you're trying to tell me is one of her lovers might help us deal with Bonaparte, is that it?'

'Precisely. I think I could manage to do that.'

132

'You!'

Coster shrugged and opened his arms as though to suggest Mlle George could not resist falling into them; he had presented himself with a few flowers at her dressing-room, and she had generously repaid him by inviting him to spend the night with her. And many other nights.

'But the best of the story is that I was leaving her two evenings ago when who do you think arrived with three of his thugs?'

'Bonaparte! Did he see you?'

'Well, our paths crossed as near as I am to you, so he probably did,' Coster said. 'At least he knows *mam'zelle* isn't giving him sole performing rights.'

'Fool! You might have been recognized from the Saint-Réjant affair and captured. You know Louis de Sol's in their hands and, worse still, they've picked up Querelle, and God alone knows what he'll tell them.'

'Then, we won't give them time to talk,' Coster replied. 'I happen to know when Bonaparte is keeping a rendezvous with Mam'zelle George.'

'When?' Cadoudal's interest suddenly heightened.

'On the fiftieth performance of *Iphigénie*. He has promised to come straight from the theatre with her.'

'When is that?' Cadoudal was now alive to the importance of Coster's information; it seemed to him the Almighty was delivering Bonaparte into their hands.

'11 February.'

Cadoudal calculated quickly. Just under three weeks. Time enough to co-ordinate the final action with Pichegru and Moreau and send someone along the Liberty Line to tell the princes to come with the next detachment of men. If they were really lucky, they might grab Murat and Savary with their master. 'We must get plans of that house,' he mused.

'Those I can draw from my head.'

'And keys. Get hold of her keys for an hour and Hozier's man will cut several sets.'

With an indulgent smile on his flat-boned face, Coster conjured three keys from a pocket and dangled them before Cadoudal. 'One for the front gate, one for the front door and one for the back gate.'

Cadoudal stared at him. He had always considered Coster a playboy but under that garish costume, that aura of perfume and those artificial curls, the man had flair and courage. Coster was grinning at him. 'If you wish to carry out a personal reconnaissance, she's at the theatre between six and eleven every night except Sunday.'

'How many servants?'

'Two — a deaf old spinster who does the cooking, and a young chit who sleeps on the top floor under the eaves and never lacks for a bedmate.'

Cadoudal looked at his silver hunter. Four o'clock. Already they were lighting the street and house lamps. A quarter of an hour through unlit back streets would take them from here to her house in Rue de Provence.

He handed Coster a cape to make him less conspicuous and they left the house separately and made their way through the slums into an area where several small mansions had sprung up just before the Revolution.

Coster led Cadoudal round Rue de la Victoire to the rear gate of Mlle George's mansion, a small, two-storey building in its own ornamental gardens and hidden by trees. Coster opened the back gate and both men crept along the tree-lined drive to the house; another drive led to the postern gate; on either side, walls two metres high shut off the property from neighbouring mansions.

As they went, Cadoudal was trying to resolve the problem of spiriting Bonaparte out of this house on the night of the strike without having to fight a pitched battle with Murat, Savary and their escort. He could hide his best Chouans in the gardens at dusk to account for the soldiers in the grounds; others would attack the escort at the front and back while Coster, Joyaux and himself dealt with Bonaparte. With scaling ladders, they could hoist him over a side wall and emerge beyond the screen of guardsmen.

'Coster, take that wall and find out what's the other side . . . you know where the gates are and if the place is guarded. We can get the owner's name tomorrow.'

'I know who it is — Rapp, one of Bonaparte's generals. Shall I try the other side?'

'No need. They'll never suspect anybody would come out of General Rapp's house with his hero bound and gagged. We go that way.'

Helping each other over the high wall, they explored the grounds, thick with trees, and the driveways to the front and rear gates. Cadoudal marked places where he could post two detachments of Chouans on the night.

Back at Mlle George's mansion, Coster pointed to the light downstairs in the basement. 'The crone's in the kitchen, so we can have a look inside.'

As though he owned the house, Coster opened the front door with his key and both men slipped inside. Not only had Bonaparte set up his young actress in her own house, he had obviously pillaged quite a few public buildings to adorn it with republican copies of Greek statues and divans, tables and chairs in the antique style Paul Barras and the Directory had made fashionable. In the half-light from chandeliers in the foyer and the oil lamp hanging over the stairwell, they crept to Mlle George's bedroom.

That stopped Cadoudal in his tracks; he had the impression of stepping into a Turkish or Mameluke general's tent; from ceiling to walls, silk curtains in green and gold stripes formed a canopy; the walls themselves were draped and festooned with the same material; divans and couches lay buried under silk cushions; the only other furniture consisted of a folding table a portable mahogany chest, a simple stool and a lyre-backed chair. At the end of the room, a four-poster bed resembled another campaign tent, swathed and veiled in striped or transparent silks.

'It reminds him of his victory in Egypt, at the Pyramids,' Coster whispered in Cadoudal's ear. 'To him, women are like everything else — a battleground with himself as a conqueror.'

They looked at the three other rooms on the first floor, then the three mansard rooms above where the maid slept. On the way back, they had reached the first-floor landing when a footfall on the stairs and the flicker of an oil lamp halted them, then sent them darting into one of the often sparsely furnished rooms to hide.

'It's the old housekeeper,' Coster whispered. They listened to her crooning and mumbling to herself as she worked in the main bedroom, then retreated downstairs.

A quarter of an hour later, as they prepared to quit their hiding-place in the grounds, the front door opened and they heard two pairs of feet on the hall floor and muted voices from one of the ground-floor salons. 'She must have finished her performance early this evening,' Coster whispered.

When Cadoudal rejoined Coster under a clump of rhododendron bushes, the lieutenant was pointing at two coaches by the front gate. They heard the hooves of cavalry horses. Soon, their attention switched to the house where a light shone from the master bedroom. A shadow took shape by the window.

'I think it's him,' Coster whispered.

Someone snapped the window open and Cadoudal saw a figure reach out to close the window shutters. At no more than thirty feet, against the light, he could not fail to recognize Bonaparte.

He caught two clicks beside him and turned to see Coster holding his left arm in front of his face as a rest for his double-barelled pistol. He was aiming at the figure leaning out the window. 'Just give me the order, *mon général*.'

'No, you fool,' Cadoudal hissed, clamping a hand round the pistol. 'We'd never get out.'

'But we'd finish the tyrant.'

'And finish the *coup d'état*, too.'

They split up to crawl past the stables and coachman's house and slither over General Rapp's wall. Emerging further down the avenue, they saw confirmation that Bonaparte was keeping his mistress company. Murat, his shadow, and several officers of the consular guard stood in a bunch round the front gate with a detachment of cavalry.

'Pity,' Coster said. 'We might never get another chance.'

'I gave my word to Artois,' Cadoudal growled. 'Anyway, with Bonaparte dead I'd never trust Moreau not to grab power and hang on to it.'

That night, in Rue Bichat, Cadoudal sat down to put the final touches to his whole operation. On 11 February, they would overpower the two servants then seize Bonaparte and his mistress when they arrived late that night. Before Murat and his consular guard could guess what had happened, Aimé Joyaux, Coster and the Gaillard brothers would have begun their run down the Liberty Line with the deposed First Consul to hand him over to the British. That would signal the beginning of the *coup d'état*.

During the following week, risking capture, he visited the most important Chouan and royalist cells to brief them about the coup and warn them the signal would come during the first two weeks in February. He gave no precise date. Gathering together his own band of officers at the Chaillot mansion he had them rehearse the abduction, even to the extent of groping through dark streets from Mlle George's house in Rue de Provence through the Saint-Denis barrier and north to join the Liberty Line at L'île-Adam.

At Chaillot, too, they held their final conference. Pichegru promised that when they had dealt with Bonaparte, he and Moreau would round up five other generals and their troops; they would surround the senate while Abbé Sieyés and thirty-five other senators would proclaim the abolition of the Consulate and the birth of a new triumvirate of Moreau, Pichegru and Cadoudal.

Cadoudal ordered Joyaux and Raoul Gaillard to make for the coast and pass a written message to Captain John Wright for Pitt and Windham in London. In this, he informed Artois everything depended on their arrival in France on or before 11 February.

Within five days, the two men had returned to announce that the Comte d'Artois and his son, the Duc de Berri, would sail from Deal in the first week of February. Cadoudal decided to travel himself to the coast to meet the princes and conduct them to the capital.

Now he could see nothing to prevent him from ending Bonaparte's reign and giving France and the French back their rightful king.

BOOK II

'Real truth is very hard for history to come by . . . What is historical truth most of the time? A convenient fable.'

Napoleon to Count Emmanuel de las Cases on Saint Helena, speaking of the Cadoudal Conspiracy.

1

Never had Bonaparte felt in better spirits as he escorted Joséphine into the vast reception room at the Tuileries for the ball to mark his return from Boulogne at the end of January 1804. He had spent two whole days touring his twelve army corps, numbering 160,000 men, with the four generals who would lead the invasion of England under his personal command. Seldom had he observed such a determined and disciplined force. Crack troops like these battle-hardened veterans would carve through the English volunteer army and take London in a week.

A few days of good weather and a clear Channel and he would make himself master of his most hated rival. Nothing could then stand between him and world conquest. As soon as the fifty men-o'-war he was building in Atlantic ports had put to sea to protect his troop flotilla, he would strike.

Claire de Rémusat came towards them and curtsied. As she rose, he saw her glance at Joséphine, a question in her eyes, which he read perfectly. Had he confessed to Joséphine about them, about their liaison? But Joséphine dispelled her doubts by taking her hand and smiling.

Claire had been with him at the little inn where he had stayed at Pont-de-Briques, near Boulogne. To seduce her, he had worked a small, tactical manoeuvre, finding two missions for her husband, a palace prefect, along the Normandy coast while he kept Claire with him.

For months he had looked at this blonde, vivacious, cultured woman of twenty-two, wondering how she would react in bed with him. Would she be kittenish, grave, roguish, impulsive? She had a slender, willowy body with small, exquisitely formed breasts and a neat ankle.

But for him she had other attractions. As Joséphine's favourite palace companion and confidante, she was privy to all her secrets, and some of his. That would heighten his sexual pleasure. And make her his accomplice as well as Joséphine's. She jumped into his bed willingly, and for three nights they made love, which she did as expertly as Joséphine, which was saying a great deal.

She teased him about his conquests — Duchâtel, Grassini, Mlle George and a dozen others. He threw in quite a few more that she had not heard of, knowing Joséphine would get wind of them and this would

146

arouse her Creole jealousy. But he also learned some home truths about Joséphine's past love affairs and her present-day philandering, which he doubted if even Fouché knew. That did not please him.

However, everything seemed to be running the right way for him, he thought, as he stepped slowly through the ranks of guests in the green and gold salon where French kings had held court for centuries. He acknowledged the applause from every side. More than a thousand candles in eight vast chandeliers lit the scene, spangling from the jewelled women and military and naval braiding, flickering across *chefs d'oeuvre* of painting and tapestry on the walls, much of it appropriated as the spoils of his foreign conquests.

In such a setting, Bonaparte could fancy himself as a modern caesar. He chatted with members of the diplomatic corps and broke stride every now and again to small talk with some minor official whose name he recalled. With that trick and his facility for memorizing names and faces, every private in his army imagined Le Petit Caporal knew his whole background and family history.

Nevertheless, his brow clouded when he noticed Talleyrand and Fouché with their heads together. Whatever those two devils had

147

to say to each other would benefit no one else, he reflected. He had sacked Fouché as police minister because the man still harboured Jacobin ideas and meant to sabotage any attempt to convert the consulate into something more permanent. He had another reason. Fouché knew too many private secrets about the Bonaparte clan.

Talleyrand, he would have sent packing with Fouché long ago because of his money-grubbing, his scheming and his womanizing, but he had yet to find anyone with half this unfrocked bishop's cunning and ability as foreign minister.

Bonaparte signalled for the ball to begin then moved among the guests. He paused to compliment several ladies on wearing more substantial dresses than the flimsy, transparent fashions which left their charms exposed to both male eyes and draughts in these cavernous palace galleries. He had often taken Joséphine to task for showing too much of herself, but she ignored his strictures. Some people affirmed he kept the heating to a minimum in his palaces to prevent women appearing in garments that left too little to guesswork.

Finally, he came face to face with Talleyrand and Fouché. His foreign minister congratulated him on his trip and his invasion strategy. 'From what I overhear, sire, our old enemy, Pitt, will soon be back in power.'

'We realized Addington was no more than a stopgap,' Bonaparte said. 'But I had hoped my friend, Charles James Fox, might have formed a government we could have treated with — for the time being.'

'Pity,' Talleyrand said, shaking his head. 'But they whisper Pitt's a sick man and can't last much longer.' He raised an imaginary glass to his lips to lend point to his statement. 'But he still has enough will-power, energy and money to try to form another coalition of Austrians and Prussians against us.'

'Only if he's quick enough to stop me from planting the French flag on the Tower of London,' Bonaparte snapped.

Fouché, who had listened without saying anything, suddenly whispered in a voice Bonaparte could hardly catch, 'I hear Monsieur Pitt has already begun his campaign against you.'

'Meaning?'

'He has already recruited Chouans and royalists and provided them with gold and arms.'

'We know all that, Fouché.'

'But did you know, Consul, the air of Paris is full of daggers, all pointed at you?'

'English daggers, I suppose.'

'Yes, Consul, English daggers blessed by French princes and in French hands.'

'So, you're still acting the policeman, Fouché!'

'I have many old friends in the strangest places,' Fouché came back, blandly.

Bonaparte realized nothing would drag another hint out of this fish-eyed spectre unless he thrust the police ministry portfolio back into his scrawny fingers. But he had not forgiven Fouché his treachery when he and Talleyrand believed rumours he had lost the Battle of Marengo in Italy nearly four years before and both of them had begun plotting to manipulate another general into the Tuileries. Probably General Jean-Victor Moreau, his great rival. No, he'd rather die assassinated than give this snake the satisfaction of foiling another plot, even one he had not fabricated.

In Fouché's place he had appointed a chief justice, Claude-Ambroise Régnier, a roly-poly man who waddled like a turtle and lost himself in judicial abstractions. Hardly the man to thwart the thirty-second plot on his life, if Fouché was right and the royalists were bent on assassinating him. He needed someone light-footed, ruthless, and obedient. But meanwhile he meant to control his own police and intelligence network.

In his short life he had mastered quite a few arts and sciences, and criminal investigation must lend itself to certain principles and calculations like any other science. If he added his experience of human nature and behaviour plus a little intuition, he could play the detective as well as Fouché.

When he had chatted to twenty or more guests he left Joséphine to do the honours and made his way along two corridors to his own first-floor suite of rooms and his study. Roustam, the Mameluke servant who had sworn eternal allegiance to him after the Battle of the Pyramids, smacked a hand on his braided chest in salute as he opened the door.

Claude-François Méneval, the new secretary his brother Joseph Bonaparte had found him was still sitting in the window embrasure scribing that afternoon's dictation, candles flaming all round him. If Méneval could call it dictation. For the secretary had discovered that the First Consul mumbled and chewed words before spitting them out in verbal shorthand with that quaint twang like volleys of musket shot. So much so that he had to leave great areas of blank space and fill them in later. However, the palace staff congratulated him as one of the few secretaries who could decipher Bonaparte's jargon through

151

his Corsican accent.

Still with Fouché's sinister hints in his ears, Bonaparte went to the nervous young man and seized the pile of letters which he scanned quickly, signed, then threw them on the floor for Méneval to retrieve and dispatch. 'Before you go, Méneval, look me out the dossier on the Chouans they've arrested in Paris since October last year and leave them on my desk. Oh! And I'd like to see the reports from our London agents — Mehée de la Touche, Grandjean, Noiret and those General Andréossy controlled when he was ambassador in England.'

Unhitching his ceremonial sword, Bonaparte dropped it on the green armchair, its upholstery daubed with ink marks where he had wiped his pen, its arms notched with his knife as mnemonics; for several minutes he wandered round the study which Marie Antoinette had used as a bedroom but which he had converted into his headquarters; his books and maps lined its panelled walls and his huge desk, filing cabinets and case of mathematical instruments left their imprint on the Aubusson carpet.

None but the most favoured penetrated this sanctuary where he meditated and planned his military campaigns and political strategy. Kicking the fire into life with his boot heel, he leaned his arms on the marble fireplace and his head on them, gazing at the flames.

Fouché never uttered an unconsidered word. So, someone was really trying to stick a dagger in him! Then, he had known for months that things were stirring in the western provinces of Brittany and La Vendée. Two weeks before, he had sent his faithful chela, General René Savary, into the region to contact prefects and informants.

'Méneval, do we know when Savary gets back from Brittany?'

Méneval's quill stopped scratching and he turned tired eyes on the First Consul.

'But General Savary has returned,' he said. 'He has been waiting for three hours in the Salon Minerva to see you.'

'Imbecile! Why didn't you say?' Bonaparte stepped briskly into the room where he held his interviews. A braided figure rose with clinking spurs to salute then incline his head. Savary stood half a head taller than Bonaparte; a long, kinked nose, thin, bloodless lips and eyes like two bits of black grapeshot gave him a sinister look; his sparse, dark hair he wore like the First Consul and Julius Caesar, brushed forward on his low forehead and salient cheekbones and plastered there in wisps. But then in everything,

General Savary aped his master, even to the clipped speech and the right hand thrust through the unbuttoned tunic.

Savary had served under General Pichegru as aide-de-camp, then under General Moreau when Pichegru fell from grace; with reckless disregard for his own life and that of others, he had distinguished himself in Egypt and Italy.

He had come to Bonaparte's notice in the worst moments of the Battle of Marengo when the French centre gave and everything was crumbling; at that instant, General Desaix appeared with 5000 grenadiers to swing the battle Bonaparte's way, but at the cost of his own life. Savary bore the dead general's body to Bonaparte, knowing him to be a great favourite. From that incident, Savary had placed his unquestioning faith in the little Corsican.

For his part, the First Consul with his superstitious credence in lucky stars and omens had given this man his trust. He also knew Savary would never let any sort of skulduggery or sleazy task stand between him and higher rank; whatever his master's bidding he would comply, asking no questions and without any moral qualms.

'So, you've come back from our Celtic tribes,' Bonaparte grunted. 'What did you learn?'

154

Savary recounted in some detail how he had visited Rennes, Brest, Nantes, Angers and La Roche as well as the other centres of revolt and had met more than a dozen of his spies and scores of prefects and minor officials. 'They all agree that something's in the wind and there's going to be an uprising.'

'How and when and how big?'

'I heard a small detachment of Chouan officers landed recently in Quiberon Bay and another in Brest to alert the men who went to ground after the pacification. They're all talking about one of the princes — Artois or Berri — taking command himself.'

'I hope they both do,' Bonaparte said, smacking a clenched fist into his palm.

His London spies had reported Artois was reviewing British troops dressed in the regalia of a Bourbon prince. Did he have the courage to lead an army into France? Bonaparte doubted this, though he wished fervently Artois would land. Most of his own renown he had won abroad — in Italy, in Egypt, in the German principalities. To crush a royalist army under a royal prince would put a jewel in his own crown just as assuredly as the severed head of Louis XVI had set the seal on the revolution.

'They were whispering the first attack would be made at Brest and when that town has fallen, the royal proclamation will be issued,' Savary said. 'Everyone was sure one of the armies would be led by Cadoudal.'

'And what am I supposed to be doing while Monsieur le Comte d'Artois is conquering Brittany and marching on Paris?'

Savary's thin lips clenched and he became grave. 'They think you will not be here any longer, *mon général.*'

'Oh!'

'Well, that is, they say the Chouans will have murdered you.'

'They've tried before, remember?'

'But this time they think they can pull off their coup.'

'With English gold and the sanction of Monsieur le Prince, I suppose,' Bonaparte said, wryly. He glared at Savary. 'Do you think they can do it?'

Savary drew himself up and clenched a hand over his sword handle. 'Only across the bodies of myself and my gendarmes,' he cried.

'Then start by putting a dozen of your gendarmes — men you can trust absolutely — into bourgeois or tradesman's clothing to guard me. And if I catch any of them looking as though he's a bodyguard, he's out of my service. Understood?'

Savary understood this included him. He

saluted and disappeared, leaving Bonaparte inhaling pinch after pinch of snuff and reflecting hard on the warning — the second that evening — that his life was threatened.

Back in his study, he signed the rest of Méneval's pile of letters, dismissed the secretary then sent General Rapp to tell Joséphine they would dine in his suite of rooms.

'Constant,' he shouted to his valet, 'I'm as hungry as I was that day at Marengo.'

Constant took the hint, sending the chef word that his master would dine, as he so often did, on Chicken Marengo, one of his favourite dishes. He hoped Joséphine was in the mood, for his master's gastronomic and sexual appetites went hand in hand.

2

When Joséphine and her daughter arrived from the ball, Bonaparte took his wife's hand and kissed it then ran a paternal hand over his stepdaughter's face. He glanced appraisingly at his wife. Maybe they were right who denied her real beauty, who pointed to her weak chin and wide nostrils and imperfect teeth. He would argue with them. They hadn't gazed into her vivid blue eyes, that iridescent blue under a kingfisher's wing, or seen the vibrant highlights in her chestnut hair, or listened to that low, mellifluous voice which had first seduced him.

And they had not known the pleasure of making love to her. Well, perhaps quite a few, perhaps too many had, though he did not let his mind dwell on that. She had really betrayed him with that young ADC, Hippolyte Charles, while he was fighting his first Italian campaign, and again when he was sweating in the desert around the Pyramids. For that treachery, he had nearly wrecked their marriage. His fondness for her two children by her first husband had saved her, they whispered. Untrue. At that point, divorce would have cost him his chance of ruling France. And he still loved Joséphine.

In some strange way he could never plumb, his destiny seemed linked with this Creole six years older than himself from the island of Martinique. Hadn't she inducted him, a young, crude, brash Corsican general, into the best of Parisian society, introducing him to what the Revolution had spared of fashionable company and helping him win command of the army of Italy?

His enemies sneered that Paul Barras, head of the Directory, had foisted Joséphine, his discarded mistress, on the naive young soldier. Again untrue. He had wanted her for herself, even knowing everything about her past. What, for instance, did an affair with General Lazare Hoche matter when both expected the guillotine which had already widowed her with two children, Eugène and Hortense?

Long before she had become his mistress, Bonaparte admired her courage. Not many aristocrats would have sent their son to him, a republican general not known for his clemency, to request the sword of his father, Alexandre de Beauharnais, an executed general. They would have dreaded the guillotine themselves.

Nobody needed telling Joséphine was an

aristocrat; they had only to watch her supple body and the fluid way she moved in that high-waisted silk dress with its six-foot train. Tonight, he noticed, she was wearing a fortune in jewels; he could not recall having seen that diamond tiara set off with a cameo; nor the heavy diamond and ruby necklace with a series of the same cameos; nor the double row of pearls which served as a belt under her breasts. Well, he'd probably get the account from some Parisian jeweller in a month's time when she thought he had forgotten, or she had coaxed him to make love before confessing. Gold melted in those slender fingers, but when he thundered at her, she chided him for a skinflint, a *grippe-sou*, and deflected his anger into desire with a caress. Adding together all her faults, he calculated he must love her very much to overlook them.

They dined in Bonaparte's salon on his favourite dish, Chicken sauté à la Marengo, created just after the battle he had all but lost, but which made him master of Italy and confirmed his rule at home; from the battlefield, Dunand, his chef, had sent out a scavenging party to scrounge food for the Consul; it had returned with eggs, tomatoes, crayfish and a small chicken out of which Dunand had concocted a dish which

Bonaparte devoured and pronounced excellent, ordering Dunand to serve it after every battle. Now, it figured on the culinary repertoire of the Tuileries, Saint-Cloud, Malmaison and everywhere the Consul dined. Tonight on its silver dish, the jointed, glazed bird swam in a rich, brown sauce surmounted by slices of sautéd truffles and surrounded by fried eggs, mushrooms, bits of crayfish and fried breadcrumbs.

Bonaparte regarded his Marengo chicken as a lucky dish and, when Constant had served them, he attacked it like someone famished. Ignoring the cutlery, he picked up pieces with his fingers to gnaw and worry them; when he forgot himself, he wiped his greasy fingers on his waistcoat or silk breeches.

'Bonaparte, you know you'll be ill if you gobble your food like that,' Joséphine murmured. He frequently woke her in the night, writhing in agony and pleading for one of her tisanes to calm his stomach.

'I might as well enjoy it,' he said with a grin. 'Savary thinks I might not eat many more dinners.'

'I never believe anything that evil man says,' Joséphine exclaimed.

'Well, this time he may be right — they're plotting to murder me.'

161

'Who?'

'Who else but your friends in the noble Quartier Saint-Germain?' he said, twitting her as he invariably did about her aristocratic circle, then smiling at the look of disbelief and apprehension on her face. Joséphine did feel scared. Six or seven years ago, during his Italian campaign, she had expected — some said even hoped — to hear every hour that he had died on the battlefield like so many young republican generals. At that time, and even during his Egyptian conquest five years before, she would have grieved him, though not for long.

Now, she shared his conviction that fate had joined them together, and she had come to love and admire this uncouth Corsican who had the courage and genius to emerge from ten years of bloody revolution as supreme ruler of France at just over thirty; yet, she often found the man she had married a daunting and awesome personality.

'But, Bonaparte, what would they gain by killing you? Surely they'd be inviting Moreau or Bernadotte or another general to take over the country?'

Those two names brought a scowl to Bonaparte's face, then he shrugged. 'Those crazy royalists think one of their gutless and

162

brainless princes will ride through Paris on a white horse and up the steps of the Tuileries to take my place.'

'Haven't they offered to make you Lord Constable of France if you step down in favour of Louis XVIII?' Joséphine asked. Secretly, she hoped Bonaparte would accept and restore the monarchy, thinking this would assure their fortune and place in the new hierarchy.

'I step down for no one,' he snapped, fixing her with his blue-grey eyes. And to imply that his destiny and his favourable deities would make him supreme, he stabbed a finger at the gilded ceiling, decorated by a pupil of his favourite painter, Jacques-Louis David, with scenes from Greek mythology. 'Of course, maybe your friends in the Saint-Germain district will make it easier for me to become the real power.'

'How would they do that by trying to murder you?'

'Just cast your mind back three years to the night of the gunpowder plot a hundred yards away. Can you see the whole opera audience standing and cheering with relief when I escaped? Now if the people who know that Bonaparte has brought them peace at home and filled their bellies thought he might disappear at the hands of a royalist assassin . . . '

Almost as though afraid to divulge his real aim, he did not round off the idea. And, listening to him, Joséphine could hardly believe he intended to usurp the Bourbons who had left their mark on French history for ten centuries.

Bonaparte toyed with his dessert, then threw down his spoon. 'Ah, that Dunand,' he lamented. 'I've told him time and again not to give me things I like too much and fatten me.' He patted the beginnings of a paunch then called the *maître d'hôtel* and ordered coffee which he drank black and sweet. Joséphine watched him fidget, interpreting the signs. When he grew restive like this, he would bid Hortense goodnight in a few minutes then hurry her down the small, twisting staircase which communicated with her own apartments.

'I'm tired, Joséphine,' he said, suddenly, giving her the cue; she quickly swallowed her coffee, kissed Hortense goodnight, took the arm he offered her gallantly and they went downstairs.

'Hurry up, *ma petite Créole*,' he said, removing her shawl and helping to unbutton her bodice which he tossed, without ceremony, on the floor, following it with her dress, underskirt, petticoat and other garments, pell-mell. He gave her bottom a playful tap and her girlish figure an appraising look as she slipped between the sheets of the four-poster, tented in silk and brocade. Within seconds, he had thrown off his own uniform, scattering tunic, shirt, trousers, boots, belt and underclothing all over the room in his haste. Then he plunged into the warmed bed to seize Joséphine in his arms.

When he had first made love to her, she did not know whether to be flattered or frightened. And now, seven years afterwards, he still took possession of her as though carrying out a frontal assault on a fortress with every weapon in his arsenal.

Whenever he made love to her as ardently, as passionately as this, she forgot all about his betrayals, his mistresses — about Laure Junot, the sly, sloe-eyed wife of General Junot, about Grassini, the plump, pigeon-breasted operatic diva, about mousy Madame Duchâtel, about his latest flame, Mlle George, even about her companion, Claire de Rémusat, whom he had summoned to Boulogne with some quaint tale about keeping her husband from fretting.

When he made love to her like this,

she forgot everything, even her own misde-
meanors with Hoche, Barras, Hippolyte
Charles and others.

'*Je t'aime avec tout mon coeur, ma petite
Créole,*' he whispered afterwards, as they
went to sleep in each other's arms.

3

Midnight had just pealed softly from the ormolu clock in his bedroom when he returned from Joséphine's suite. Roustam, the Mameluke, and Constant had kept his hot bath ready at the right temperature, waiting for him as they did every night, here or at his other residences. He immersed himself in the steaming, perfumed water. For hours at a stretch he would lie soaking in hot water, and in these hours when he had rested and felt relaxed and Paris slept, his best thoughts came. His midnight mind, he called it.

Passing through his study, he had noticed Méneval had left him three bulky packets of papers on the *guéridon* — the police and ministry of justice reports on the Chouans arrested in Paris and thought to be involved in royalist plots, also the espionage files about subversive activity of French royalists in England.

Constant came to soap and scrub him then left him alone. Bonaparte focused his mental concentration on the dossiers which he had already scanned several times; his mind, which they compared to a vast filing system, sifted the names and events in those reports, searching for some common thread.

It must all connect with that gnome, Saint-Réjant, and his gunpowder plot. And that had begun where? London, wasn't it? Where royalists like Hyde de Neuville and that homespun general, Cadoudal, had gone into hiding with the princes. Fouché had sent that profligate spy of his — Mehée de la Touche — there to probe, and he'd seen Artois and Berri meeting all sorts of people, including Cadoudal, and having secret conversations with Pitt and his two war secretaries, Windham and Dundas.

Those Bourbon princes had met somebody else who had already figured in an attempted restoration and might even try again: General Charles Pichegru. From as far back as his adolescence, Bonaparte remembered the tall, powerful and intelligent monitor who had introduced him to maths and science. Hadn't Mehée and Andréossy, the former ambassador, mentioned several meetings between Pichegru and the three British statesmen at the House of Commons and Pitt's club in St James's?

Bonaparte's mind went back seven years to 1797 when he had conquered Venice and the city had handed over a royalist agent, the Comte d'Entraigues, and a trunkful of papers. Ferreting in those documents, he had discovered evidence of the conspiracy between Pichegru, the renowned general, and the Bourbon princes for the overthrow of the Directory and the restoration of the monarchy. And, curiously, General Moreau, who had known about these intrigues months before, kept quiet until he, Bonaparte, had placed the papers before the Directory!

Pichegru and the princes. Of course! And that linked with the spies' reports of several meetings between Pichegru and Cadoudal, the Breton general, in London. From this and the information Savary had uncovered, he assumed Pichegru would operate in Paris with the princes while Cadoudal raised the royal standard in Brittany and La Vendée.

When he had pondered the problem, scanning every facet, he rose and let Constant wrap him in a bathrobe. A log fire burned in his study and he stretched out on a sofa in the warmth of the flames with the pile of papers within reach. As he read through them, he realized that perhaps the plotters had gone further with their plans for a *coup d'état* than he imagined. For instance, an intercepted letter from a Chouan general, de Bar, to Cadoudal mentioned one of the princes as leading a national rebellion soon.

His eye travelled down the list of several

169

dozen royalists lying in the dungeons of the Carmes and Temple prisons; most belonged to noble families from the west and had already endured mental and physical torture without yielding even a hint of their aims or the names of their accomplices.

This man, Louis de Sol, for instance. Every attempt to make him talk had failed because the Chouan showed more courage and resolution than Chief Justice Régnier and his dull-witted subordinates. A man with a cause, Bonaparte thought. No point in torturing him to death, or others who shared his faith and fanaticism.

How had he won most of his great battles? By meticulous planning, organization and good reconnaissance; by pinning the enemy where he chose, picking its weak spot and throwing everything — cannonballs, mortar bombs, bullets and bayonets — at it until it ceded, exposing the vital centre; by keeping opposing generals baffled with unexpected tactics; by sheer speed and weight of manoeuvre by selecting the right generals and inspiring them to die rather than give an inch.

Where would he find the weak spot here? Where was that someone who would crack under pressure in this bunch of prisoners? As he scanned the list, one name sprang to his mind like an augury: Jean-Pierre Querelle.

Arrested nearly three months before because he had written to his brother-in-law asking for facts about Chouan strength, republican forces and church influence in Brittany. Querelle had stalled and bluffed during his interrogation, yet Bonaparte felt this man would talk, given the right treatment. What was a former naval surgeon, up to his eyes in debt, doing with a bunch of Chouans? He wasn't like de Sol, prepared to martyr himself for a king; a money-grubber or an intriguer more likely.

Bonaparte rang for Constant, ordering him to wake Méneval. When his secretary appeared, bleary-eyed and pale, and took his place in the embrasure, Bonaparte dictated: *'To Chief Justice Régnier and General Murat.*

The following men will be indicted and tried before a military court with conspiring against the state, with sedition and with espionage on behalf of an enemy, namely England.' He listed five prisoners three of whom had spent more than a year in prison, plus de Sol and Querelle.

From his personal files, Bonaparte drew another list of a dozen names, prominent men whom he considered recruiting to his staff. Who among these had the flair to break down determined men during interrogation?

171

Who knew something of the counter-revolutionary movements and the men who inspired them? Who had everything to fear if the Bourbons returned? One by one he eliminated the candidates until a single name remained:

Pierre-François Réal.

Like Fouché an old Jacobin, Réal had voted Louis XVI's death then followed his hero and leader, Georges Danton, into prison during Robespierre's Reign of Terror, but somehow he had escaped the guillotine. So many people Bonaparte respected had spoken glowingly of his talent as a prosecutor, his integrity, his fine intellect. Réal's republican background would appease the revolutionaries and mask the fact that Bonaparte was meditating the formation of a new dynasty — his own.

Later that morning, Réal answered his summons. Bonaparte studied this quiet, dignified man with his innocent look and blue eyes and could see how he might win the confidence of accused men then have them convicted; he realized why some people considered him less honest than his face and branded him as foxy.

Flattered by the First Consul's interest in him, Réal accepted the job of state councillor for internal security. Bonaparte explained his suspicions that a plot against the state and his own life was hatching in the royalist camp, that Brittany and La Vendée were preparing an uprising; he had therefore decided to try five royalist prisoners to find out if they would confess their part in the plot under threat of death, for every one of them would be condemned.

In the meantime, his government would prepare public opinion against these royalist attempts to destroy order in the country. He himself would address the senate in a day or two.

He told Réal, 'I shall proclaim the odious conduct of the British Government which has thrown on to our shores these monsters whom it has paid and fed during the peace with the intention of assassinating the lawful ruler of France.'

He ringed one of the five names. 'This man, Querelle, may be the key. I have a feeling he knows something vital. If we let him have a good look at his firing squad it might loosen his tongue.'

At Bonaparte's instigation, General Murat picked the tribunal which sat on 26 January — several days after the meeting between Pichegru, Moreau and Cadoudal in Paris. Two of the men, a royalist adjutant-general Picot, and an innkeeper, le Bourgeois, admitted they had entered France more than a year before to kill the First Consul, but they would reveal nothing else, neither where they came from nor who had ordered and paid them. Pichegru? Cadoudal? They knew nothing of these men or about any alleged *coup d'état*. Murat's tribunal got nowhere with de Sol and the other royalist, Monsieur de Pioger, who both stonewalled, argued, demanded proof of their so-called sedition, spying and attempted assassination and showed such vehemence the court had to acquit them, against Bonaparte's wishes. Yet they both returned to Bicêtre Prison to remain at the government's disposal.

Querelle put on a brave face, denying everything. For months he had double-talked his way through every interrogation and knew they had little or no proof against him. But this time, on the say-so of Bonaparte, the tribunal found him guilty and sentenced him to death by firing squad. Even then, the pock-marked little man bore up as they took him to the death-cell in the Abbaye Prison with Picot and Le Bourgeois.

Murat brought news of the trial to Bonaparte in his audience room, entering with his shako glittering under his arm and his tunic sagging under the weight of gold braid. Such flamboyance irritated the First

174

Consul, and only Murat's reckless bravery in battle pardoned his extravagant style. Murat had the dark, glistening curly hair and golden complexion of a gypsy which had appealed more to his wife, Caroline Bonaparte, than to her brother who had nearly forbade her marriage to this son of an innkeeper.

When Murat had ended his report, Bonaparte looked at him then said, 'Now listen hard. Let this man, Querelle, stew for several hours then put on a rehearsal of his own execution.'

'How?' Murat queried, his face darkening at such an idea, for though brave he neither liked shedding blood off the battlefield, nor the idea of mentally torturing a condemned man.

'Use your wits. Give him a window seat when you shoot the others.'

Murat had to obey. For hours, Querelle sat petrified in his grim cell with its barred windows level with the courtyard where he witnessed the preparations for the execution of Adjutant-General Picot and Le Bourgeois, both unconcerned as they watched beside him. Again and again, the platoon went through its execution drill until Querelle felt sick. Yet, when his two companions quit the death-cell and reappeared in the courtyard, his horrified eyes tracked every movement

175

through the slit windows; he saw and heard the two men refuse blindfolds and the crowd on the prison walls howling for blood.

As the platoon of soldiers raised their muskets, Querelle could no longer bear to look. His nerve broke. He buried his head in his arms and squatted on the flagstones of his cell. A minute later when the volleys rang out, then the four *coups de grâce* he began to convulse and scream so deliriously that the jailers called the doctor who administered bromide. Querelle caught hold of the medical officer and began babbling about a plot to kill Bonaparte with Chouan leaders behind it. 'I don't want to die,' he sobbed to the doctor who advised him to confess all this to General Murat, Governor of Paris. Which Querelle did.

On receiving this message, Murat drove at once to the Tuileries where Bonaparte was conferring with Réal.

'Querelle wants to confess.'

Bonaparte stopped pacing the salon, held out a hand into which Constant put a full snuffbox; he took two pinches then fixed his eyes on Murat and Réal as much as to say, 'I told you so.'

Aloud, he ordered Murat, 'All right, leave him for another hour and keep your firing squad making the right noises outside his

176

cell.' He turned to Réal. 'You go and question him in an hour's time, but promise him nothing. No reprieve. No pardon. His kind doesn't deserve it. When you've heard what he has to say he'll be shot.'

'But, *mon général* — ' Murat began.

'No buts.'

And he waved both men out of the salon and disappeared into his study where he resumed his dictation of new battle orders to the generals commanding the invasion forces grouped around Boulogne.

He had finished his paperwork and was sitting in a chair, letting Constant shave him when Réal returned. From the councillor's grave look and pale complexion, Bonaparte assumed he had just witnessed his first execution by firing squad.

'He's dead, is he?' he snapped.

'No, Consul — and a good job for you and me.'

'What do you mean?' Catching Réal's glance towards Constant, he said, 'You can speak freely — what happened?'

'Cadoudal is in Paris.'

Bonaparte put up a hand to halt Constant's razor then to stop Réal from making further remarks while he dismissed the valet. It even seemed to Réal he crossed himself before motioning him into the study.

'Cadoudal in Paris? I don't believe it,' he muttered. He paused, recalling that day four years ago when he had argued with Cadoudal in the next room and had even imagined the Breton giant meant to strangle him with his bare hands. 'How long does Querelle say he's been here?'

'Six months, Consul. And he has a gang with him.'

Six months. Had a Chouan execution squad been prowling around him for all that time and none of his policemen any the wiser? He listened, incredulously, as Réal recounted the evidence he had wrung from the terrified Querelle; he had a list of names that signified nothing, though Bonaparte assumed they were *noms de guerre*, for Cadoudal and his band.

Querelle had told how they had arrived by British cutter and roughly where they had disembarked; he had since seen none of his companions but had received messages and his pay under a stone on the waste ground of the Champs Elysées; he recognized de Sol as one of the men who had smuggled Cadoudal into Paris.

'They've been here all that time,' Bonaparte interjected. 'So, what were they waiting for?'

'Querelle mentioned they were waiting for orders.'

'Orders from whom and where? Go back and ask him that, and keep pumping him until he spills everything, everything — even if you have to torture him. And while you're about it, lean hard on this man de Sol.' Bonaparte took several pinches of snuff, wiping his nose on his tunic sleeve in his excitement. 'De Sol knows almost everything and that abject rogue Querelle knows only what he has overheard.' He pointed a finger at Réal. 'And you, Councillor Réal, only know a quarter of this whole business. Keep me in touch with everything you learn; everything, you understand?'

He rapped out new instructions for Réal. When he had squeezed Querelle dry, they must send a strong detachment of gendarmes along the route between Paris and the coast to identify the relay posts he mentioned. 'But the essential thing is to find that disembark-ation point as quickly as possible,' Bonaparte said. 'Immediately they've located it I must be informed.'

Now that Querelle had broken, he con-fessed everything, although his information remained sketchy. But de Sol refused to talk even when they subjected him to torture and deprived him of food and water. Threatened with summary execution, he shrugged. Con-fronted with the pathetic figure of Querelle, de Sol laughed in his face then scoffed at Réal and his interrogators, saying, 'A wretch like that, condemned to death, cannot give legal evidence.' For want of proof, they had to annul de Sol's sentence and send him back to prison.

Querelle attempted to retrace the route from Paris to the coast while Réal sent a group of gendarmes to Le Tréport to search for the first stage of the relay line; it took Querelle some weeks before he identified the house at Saint-Leu, near Paris, where they had spent a night; at the other end, Gaston Troche, the clockmaker, and his son were arrested.

Soon, the Temple Prison was filling with royalists and bewildered innkeepers who thought they were sheltering petty criminals or bankrupt tradesmen on the run.

By then, nothing much remained of Cadoudal's Liberty Line.

4

General René Savary sensed that something momentous was happening when General Rapp escorted him briskly into Bonaparte's study and sanctuary. To his astonishment, he discovered the First Consul lying full-length on the Aubusson carpet with maps scattered all round him; on one he was toiling with a pair of compasses and protractors. When Savary's spurs clinked as he brought his heels together and saluted, Bonaparte bounded to his feet, clutching a map which he spread across his huge desk. Savary noticed he had drawn almost a straight line from the Saint-Denis Gate through Beauvais to the Channel coast just above Dieppe. Along this line, daubed with snuff marks, Bonaparte had ringed places like L'Île-Adam, Saint-Lubin, Auteuil, Aumale, Preusseville, Le Tréport with times and distances noted for the average horseman and man on foot.

'Savary, you're the one man I can trust with perhaps the most important assignment since I became consul,' Bonaparte said. Such a compliment brought a flush to Savary's face; his master had promoted him to brigadier-general last year and he could see at least a third star glittering on his kepi soon. 'Can you keep a secret, Savary — a vital secret?'

'To the death and beyond, *mon général*.'

'Since last summer they've landed at least fifty Chouans and probably a hundred or more on those cliffs.' Bonaparte rammed his compass points into the line of *falaise* around Le Tréport. 'And they've come with orders to murder me.'

'That they'll never do.'

'They must have had their chances,' Bonaparte snapped.

'They'll pay for them.'

Bonaparte pointed to the line on the map. 'This is their relay route between Paris and the coast and England,' he said, announcing each of the names they had discovered.

However, they had not yet located the exact spot where Cadoudal and his men had scaled the cliffs and he assumed they had split their relay line into five or six tributaries near the coast to make it more difficult for anyone to discover. 'Take the best of your gendarmes and find that point on the cliffs where they got through.' Bonaparte shook his head in bewilderment. 'How did they do it with an army of a hundred and sixty thousand men camped along that coast and the navy patrolling the Channel?' he mused aloud.

'You shall have the answer in a day or two, sire,' Savary replied. 'I shall leave within the hour.'

'Take that clockmaker's son, Troche, whom they arrested the other day. He knows the spot. And Querelle.'

Savary saluted and was halfway to the door when Bonaparte stopped him. 'I haven't finished,' he barked. 'Nor have I told you what it's all about.' He began to quarter the room with that jinking stride, halting every few seconds as though his feet were punctuating his train of thought. 'When you identify the landing site, do nothing, but have at least a hundred armed and trusted men with you.'

'They'll come ashore in force then, *mon général*?'

Bonaparte shook his head. 'They'd be mad, with a whole invasion army to meet them. No, they'll sneak ashore . . . I expect there'll be one cutter which will put between ten and twenty men on to the beach once it gets the signal.'

'Signal?'

'That's another of your tasks. Troche, or someone around there, knows the landing signal. Arrest them, whoever they are, and force them to signal that English cutter to put its passengers on French soil.'

'Do I attack them?'

'On no account. Allow them to scale the cliffs then take them alive. Alive, you understand?'

Savary nodded. 'And the English ship?'

'Admiral Villeneuve has orders to deal with that the moment it has discharged its passengers.'

Gradually, it was dawning on Savary's limited intelligence that the First Consul knew who was landing from the British cutter. 'Is it . . . is it one of the Bourbons?' he whispered.

'That's the secret you have to keep,' Bonaparte said. 'The truth is we don't know precisely, but I'm guessing they sent for the princes before they tried to assassinate me and stage their *coup d'état*.'

'You mean the Chouans were going to try to put a Bourbon back on the throne here?' Savary gasped.

'Are going to try,' Bonaparte corrected.

'Just let them,' Savary growled, then added, 'What wouldn't I give to get my hands on a Bourbon prince!'

'No more than I'd give,' Bonaparte said through his teeth. 'Now we have our chance.' He dismissed Savary with a wave of his hand

and an injunction to keep him informed every day by special courier.

Bonaparte went back to his calculations. He was humming, tunelessly, 'La Marseillaise', a sign he was happy. Indeed, he felt in his element, pulling together all the strands of this plot, even though it was aimed at his own life. He alone knew where it might lead. Neither Savary nor Réal nor anyone else realized what a vital role a live Bourbon prince leading a revolt with the collusion of the enemy could play in the destiny of Napoleon Bonaparte and France.

To him, believing as he did in his lucky star and in the ironies of history, it seemed the conspirators were unwittingly plotting to help him consecrate his rule and assure his dynasty.

5

At first, Cadoudal could not believe the news that Hozier and Bouvet brought him. Yet, it came from two separate sources, one of them an old servant of Marie de Saint-Leger now working in the Tuileries kitchens, the other a corporal with royalist sympathies on guard duty at the Saint-Denis Gate. General René Savary, it seemed, had ridden north the previous evening, 5 February, with a strong detachment of gendarmes. With them had gone two prisoners, one of whom had a pock-marked face and a beaky nose.

'Querelle!' Cadoudal shouted.

Charles d'Hozier nodded. 'That's what we're afraid of,' he murmured, pulling a copy of the official *Le Moniteur* from his pocket and handing it to Cadoudal. There, he read that Jean-Pierre Querelle had confessed to conspiring against the state and its rulers.

'We didn't give it credence at first,' Hozier said. 'We thought Bonaparte might be trying to scare us off or flush us into the open. But with the information from the Tuileries and the barrier we reckoned it must be true.'

'It is true,' Cadoudal growled. 'And the

princes will be at sea today or tomorrow.'

'What!' Hozier and Bouvet cried together.

'That's why Savary's gone and that's who Bonaparte is after.'

Cadoudal paced up and down the narrow bedroom. 'Querelle will identify one of the relay stations and soon Bonaparte will have the whole Liberty Line and they'll be waiting at Biville to grab the Comte d'Artois and the Duc de Berri.' His broad face was working with rage. 'It's my fault . . . the one man I should have left behind, and he's betrayed us all.'

'Never mind, Georges,' Hozier said. 'Somehow, we must warn the princes.'

Cadoudal nodded. He dispatched Bouvet to fetch Raoul Gaillard in Notre Dame des Champs; he gave the Norman instructions to ride north changing mounts every ten miles and keeping clear of the line. Between Beauvais and Rouen, at a place called Gournay-en-Bray he would find the Chevalier de Cacqueray and merely say, 'The secret's out, you know what you have to do.'

With his two lieutenants, Cadoudal made the rounds, warning everyone to keep off the streets and away from rendezvous points, cafés and other public places; he sent two men into Brittany and La Vendée to instruct Chouan leaders like Saint-Hilaire to stand

187

down their men. Few people knew he had alerted the princes, so he mentioned the danger they were running only to Pichegru. Since Querelle might have heard something about the Chaillot mansion he gave orders to evacuate it. Assembling his principal officers, he advised them to change their hiding-places and operate as individuals from that moment. If they managed to save the princes, they would try again in several months when things had calmed down.

'If the princes are captured, Bonaparte will have them shot,' Pichegru said. 'He's only waiting to take the blood of a royal prince to convince the republicans the Bourbons are finished.'

'He'll shoot them over our corpses,' Cadoudal retorted.

For two days he waited and wondered before Raoul Gaillard returned with the news he had contacted the Chevalier de Cacqueray who had jumped on a horse and made for the coast to warn the British cutter. 'I don't know if he would get there,' Gaillard said.

'Any word of Savary and his troops?'

'Only that they'd reached the Poterie the day I passed the message.'

'So the line's gone,' Cadoudal groaned. 'I've never wished anybody dead more than that traitor Querelle.' He prayed Cacqueray had arrived in time to warn the cutter. Never would he forgive himself if he had led Artois and Berri into a trap set by Bonaparte.

That week forced him to remember what Pichegru had said about Bonaparte's flair for police work, for so many blows fell that he was convinced the little Corsican had duped them all and they had blundered into his trap.

On 8 February, his own orderly, Louis Picot, came to the Cloche d'Or to demand instructions. As he rapped out their signal on the shutter several policemen surrounded him; he drew his pistol and fired, but missed. Two other Chouans fell into the same ambush and were locked up with Picot, the innkeeper Denant and his wife. Worse still, the police unearthed bills and other evidence which led them to Rue Saintonge where they caught Coster-Saint-Victor and Michel Roger, both almost essential to the operation.

Then came the cruellest blow — Bouvet's arrest. His predilection for women lost him. An anonymous letter, probably written by one of his discarded mistresses, denounced Marie de Saint-Leger as a royalist conspirator; soon the police had traced the renting of the Chaillot mansion to her, also her address in Rue Bellechasse.

Despite Cadoudal's warning to stay in hiding, Bouvet continued to call at Rue

Bellechasse. On 12 February, he stumbled into a police ambush there. Locked in a room, Bouvet managed to bribe the inspector guarding him and burn personal papers and other evidence before they took him, manacled, to the police prefecture in Rue Jerusalem. He began by denying everything, even the evidence uncovered at his Pontoise house by Inspector Pierre-Jean Pasques. But that interrogation scared and confused him, and he spent the night in a grim cell at the Temple Prison.

★   ★   ★

Next morning, Bouvet woke in a fit of depression. Had they really discovered everything? They had quizzed him about Pichegru and Cadoudal, cited places along the Liberty Line and knew about the London end of the plot. He spent all that morning in bleak thought. How could he face the mental and physical anguish of a long inquisition, trial, life imprisonment, or the guillotine? Why didn't he end it here and now, in this dingy cell?

After that, his mind became turmoil of doubt and fear in which fact and fantasy were confused. He heard a voice — his own? — threaten suicide in the presence of his

190

gaoler, a shambling villain with the most evil face he had ever seen. They had come to interrogate him and he recalled fragments of question and response, but like a bad dream.

He knew nothing real until he woke up in the prison office, babbling. There, they told him he had knotted two handkerchiefs together, slung this makeshift noose round the top of a heavy wardrobe, stood on the bed, put his head through and jumped off. Savart, the gaoler, had returned just in time to cut him down and carry him to the office where they had succeeded in saving his life.

But they had worse news for him. In his delirium, he had raved about a plot and a *coup d'état* and had mentioned people by name, among them General Pichegru.

Cadoudal knew of Bouvet's arrest though nothing about his confession. However, he and Joyaux changed their hideouts and warned Pichegru and the other leaders to find safe houses until they heard what had happened to the arrested men. They might have to lie low for months until Bonaparte's police had lost trace of them.

Only one thing worried Cadoudal: the fate of the princes whom he had unwittingly led into a trap.

6

With two wagonloads of gendarmes and Troche and Querelle for guides, General Savary reached Dieppe where he commandeered another fifty soldiers. His prisoners then pointed him towards the farm at Guilmecourt where Cadoudal and his Chouans had spent their first night. At the Poterie, they arrested the farmer, Jacques Détrimont and his family, and Laurent Duflot, one of the three men who understood the system of coded signals with the English warships. But Duflot and the others resisted threats and promises to make them talk and denied every accusation with which Troche tried to trap them and save his own neck. Even when Savary had discovered the scaling rope on the Biville cliff, they still professed ignorance of its purpose.

Three days before, the Chevalier de Cacqueray had dodged through the republican lines, his red cloak tattered by musket shot, with his message from Cadoudal; he had chanced on Duflot and warned him that Bonaparte's troops were setting an ambush for the British cutter and he must ensure no one landed. But how? Duflot wondered, as he lay under guard at the farmhouse.

Fortunately, the weather and Troche's treachery solved his problem. On the bare cliff, snow had fallen and a gale was battering them with waves, and drenching Savary's soldiers with spray as they lay peering through the blizzard to scan the Channel.

At midday on 7 February, the wind dropped suddenly and Savary spotted two British cutters standing off three miles from the coast under stay-sails, their mainsails and jibs reefed. He could hardly believe his luck. Yet, as he watched for the rest of that short winter day, the cutters merely tacked back and forth over the same stretch of water, their signal lamps flashing from time to time.

'They're waiting for a signal,' Savary muttered. 'Troche, didn't you say something about three men who knew the signals.'

'Duflot's one of them.'

'Fetch him,' Savary ordered.

Duflot arrived, affirming he knew nothing of any system of signals. But yes, he had once seen somebody signalling out to sea from these cliffs and he could try to imitate the signals. No fool, the young Chouan noticed the storm was blowing up again. Who could

193

blame him if the ships decided to postpone their landing? He should have flashed his lantern three times until receiving an answer from the cutters; instead, he held it aloft signifying danger.

One of the ships turned its bows towards the shore and hoisted its sail. Savary rubbed his gloved hands as he tracked the vessel through a spyglass towards the shoreline. Young Duflot shivered, thinking he had lured the ship into a trap. But a mile offshore, the cutter suddenly put its helm about and fired a broadside informing Duflot it had understood his message.

Several hours later, one of the cutters headed downwind, away from the coast. Savary swore. In this weather, Admiral Villeneuve had no chance of catching and boarding these lightweight craft. And he could hardly blame Duflot when no one could have landed passengers with such high seas running. For three more days, the second cutter zig-zagged back and forth, firing a broadside every four hours; but Duflot kept warning it to keep clear and finally it, too, put about on 11 February and followed the first ship up-channel.

Savary watched it — and his chance of that third star — disappear. More than ever he felt it had one or both Bourbon princes aboard.

Furious he returned to report personally to the First Consul on 13 February.

Never in more than three years of close collaboration had he seen Bonaparte so angry.

7

Bouvet de Lozier opened his eyes in a room of the prison hospital, still suffering from his nightmare ordeal and the massive dose of bromides they had fed him. His mind wandered through a bewildering maze trying to sift out some fragments of reality. Had he felt hands round his neck while they hammered questions at him? Or had he genuinely tied his cravat and handkerchief together and tried to hang himself? Had he heard that evil, leering Savart (who, they said, took his orders from a bigger blackguard, General Savary) threaten to murder him? Bouvet's throat felt on fire and his ears buzzed. As the room dropped slowly into shape around him he caught sight of a familiar figure — François Réal.

'*Mon pauvre ami*,' Réal began. 'The last of the many times we met was at Madame de Staël's salon, or was it *chez* Madame de Genlis?' He shook his head in sorrow. 'And to think I should meet you here.' Réal omitted to mention he had become Bonaparte's councillor for state security.

Bouvet wept to see a friend, someone of his

own circle and background. Réal comforted him, suggesting Bouvet should confide in him as a friend. Too light-headed to suspect a trap, Bouvet began to ramble, prompted from time to time by Réal, unaware someone was scribing their conversation. As his recollection returned, Bouvet's rancour against General Moreau mounted; before he realized what was happening, he had revealed almost the whole conspiracy, blaming Moreau for playing a double game by luring the Chouans and royalists to Paris to rid the country of the First Consul then seize power for himself

When he had croaked and whispered everything, Réal hurried to the Tuileries to put Bouvet's signed deposition before Bonaparte. All the First Consul's wrath at the loss of his Bourbon princes evaporated. He had a bigger prize: his arch rival Moreau. It confirmed his intuition that this whole conspiracy revolved around Moreau's Club; and here, thanks to this Bouvet de Lozier, aristocrat and self-styled adjutant-general of the royalist army, he had proof of Moreau's link with Pichegru and the Bourbon princes. Another nail in the Bourbon coffin, another gemstone for the crown he was making for himself. Bonaparte revelled in this game of plot and counter-plot. Eyes glinting, he read Bouvet's confession:

It is a man saved from death's door and still in the shadow of death who demands vengeance against those whose perfidy has thrown him and his party into the abyss where he now lies.

Sent to support the Bourbon cause he finds himself forced to fight for Moreau or renounce the enterprise that was the whole object of his mission.

To explain: Monsieur le Prince (Artois) had to come to France to set himself at the head of the royalist party: Moreau promised to join the Bourbon cause. Once the royalists had come to France, Moreau retracted; he proposed they should work for him and have him named dictator.

Bonaparte had all he needed. But, for good measure, his royalist prisoner had named General Pichegru, his aide General Lajolais, Georges Cadoudal and others in the plot. However, he did state Cadoudal had promised to await the arrival of the Bourbon princes before striking at the First Consul and mounting the *coup d'état*. One door shuts, another opens, Bonaparte thought. A blueblood like this crumples and vomits everything when the Temple gaolers apply a little persuasion. They had been scorching the feet and crushing the thumbs of Cadoudal's illiterate batman, Picot, for weeks and he had demonstrated greater faith and courage.

Bonaparte threw the papers on his desk. 'What did I tell you, Réal — you didn't know a quarter of the story? Now you know half and I doubt if you'll ever find the other half.'

'Are we going to arrest Moreau?'

'We have enough evidence to shoot or guillotine him, but leave it a day or two.' And he gestured Réal out of the study before turning again to the confession papers.

They gave him much to ponder. After himself, Moreau ranked as the most popular man in France. Nobody, not even a Bonaparte, arrested someone of his standing without considering its effects on the Paris streets and in army barracks throughout the land. They would accuse him of suppressing his one competitor through jealousy or fear or both.

'Take a note,' he muttered to Méneval, who jerked into action to record a summons of the state council — Bonaparte's fellow-consuls, Jean-Jacques Cambacérès and Charles-François Lebrun, Talleyrand, Régnier, Réal, several other ministers and councillors.

As an afterthought, he added one name that made even Méneval blink. 'Yes, I did say Fouché,' he snapped, when the secretary queried the name. Not that he needed Fouché's or the council's advice, but if he meant to arrest Moreau, he must have full backing. A man like Fouché knew how the republicans would react to the indictment of one of their heroes. He might also need that royalist file which Fouché had cunningly taken with him, like so many other secret papers, when he quit the ministry of police.

★   ★   ★

Later that evening, he wandered into Joséphine's yellow salon, sat down by the fire and picked up his little nephew, Napoleon, child of his brother, Louis, and Hortense, Joséphine's daughter. Although he was dandling the infant on his knee and teasing him, Joséphine sensed his troubled mind, but she went on dressing for dinner, aware he would eventually blurt it out.

'I'm going to arrest Moreau,' he said, suddenly, and noted the look of horror that crossed her face. 'I know,' he said, 'it'll set the whole country by the ears and they'll sneer I'm jealous. Me jealous! When I left him my best army for Hohenlinden and fought Marengo with raw recruits.' Observing Joséphine's eyes film over, he put down the child and went to console her. 'There's no cause to cry,' he murmured, running a hand over her face then wiping away a tear halted in its track by her rouge.

'It's what they'll whisper about you that makes me cry,' she sobbed.

'All right, let them gossip. How can I shut my eyes to what he has done? I have proof he's been plotting with the royalists and several senators, and he'll be judged fairly like anybody else.'

'But they'll say I egged you on because I'm jealous of his wife.'

'Well, aren't you? Didn't she try to usurp your place at Saint-Cloud during that banquet several months ago?' Then he added, maliciously, 'And she's very pretty.'

Joséphine rose to the bait, a flush showing through her thick rouge. 'She's a bitch who thinks she's the queen of her little court in Rue d'Anjou and one day she'll be sitting here in my place.'

'So you see, *ma petite Créole*, I'm right to order Moreau's arrest,' he said, smiling. She saw he had manoeuvred her, as he did everybody, round to his own way of thinking. Nobody ever won an argument with Bonaparte.

★　★　★

201

Next morning, he greeted each member of his emergency state council as they took their places at the vast horseshoe conference table in the Tuileries. Intrigued, he watched Talleyrand and Fouché bow to each other, though only from the nape of their necks and without a glimmer of emotion on their plaster-cast features. What had they said of each other?

'Monsieur Fouché scorns men because he has doubtless studied himself closely,' Talleyrand had commented.

'The only vice he lacked,' Fouché murmured, when Talleyrand became vice-president of a learned society.

Before taking his seat, Fouché stopped to whisper, 'Consul, you have been within a few feet of death at least a dozen times.'

'Oh! Where?'

'Among other occasions at the house of a young lady in Allée des Veuves, then three weeks ago in Rue de Provence and again when reviewing the guard last week.'

Bonaparte shrugged, trying to look unimpressed although Fouché's remarks had shaken him. He declared the proceedings open and had Réal outline the evidence he and his police had garnered in the last week, explaining how the conspirators had recruited Moreau through his old army chief, Pichegru.

'Do we know for certain Pichegru is in Paris?' Cambacérès asked.

'Yes,' Bonaparte replied. 'I remembered myself he had a brother in orders, Abbé Jean-Louis Pichegru, so I sent someone to question him. The *abbé* admitted he had seen Pichegru and warned him against taking part in any plot. But he spoke too late. We shall find him.'

Chief Justice Régnier rested his paunch on the table as he intoned Bouvet de Lozier's statement linking Pichegru with Moreau and therefore with the Chouan and royalist conspirators.

'Your police did very well, sire, to take the noose off his neck just in time,' Talleyrand murmured, blandly.

'What do you mean? He tried to hang himself.'

'Strange things happen in prisons,' the foreign minister replied. 'You know what people are. They'll say we squeezed his windpipe to make his tongue wag.'

'Harmless gossip,' Bonaparte snapped. 'Whatever they did, this man admits he was present at the meeting between Moreau, Pichegru and that thug, Cadoudal. He affirms they were plotting not only against me, but against the state.'

'You may have a hard job convincing a

military tribunal that Moreau is backing the Bourbons,' said Cambacérès, the Second Consul. A Montpellier lawyer and a member of the original revolutionary convention, he voiced his fear the public might misinterpret the First Consul's motives.

'So I should do nothing,' Bonaparte said, sarcastically.

'No, you must arrest him,' Talleyrand put in. 'Moreau has had contact with known conspirators and agents of a country with which we are at war.'

Others echoed his opinion, giving Bonaparte the consensus he needed to endorse his own decision. Only Fouché had not uttered. Bonaparte was looking at him when General Rapp entered with a message. When Bonaparte had run an eye over it, he passed it to Fouché. 'Have you met either of these names before?' he asked.

'Michel Roger, no. But Coster-Saint-Victor was involved in the Saint-Nicaise plot and fled to America before we could arrest him.'

'Well, we have now. He was picked up with Roger in Rue Saintonge last night.'

'How many royalist have you caught?'

'Twenty-three,' Réal said.

'And there are more than two hundred Chouans and well over six hundred armed royalists ready to strike in Paris alone,' Fouché murmured, in that neutral whisper which chilled everyone round the table.

'They really do mean to kill you, sire,' Talleyrand said.

'My life means nothing, but the state does.'

'But you are the state,' Talleyrand retorted.

'We're wasting time arguing,' Bonaparte snapped. 'We must strike at the head of this conspiracy. We must arrest Moreau then draft every available policeman and gendarme into the hunt for the other two leaders, Pichegru and Cadoudal.'

'I wonder why they held their hand so long?' Fouché murmured.

'Yes, why have they waited more than six months to strike?' Cambacérès asked.

'I'll tell you why,' Bonaparte said. 'They're expecting one of their Bourbon princes to come and give their assassination and their *coup d'état* the gloss of legality.'

'Which prince?' Talleyrand asked. 'I didn't think any of them had the courage.'

'No, they send their thugs to do what they're too cowardly to do themselves,' Bonaparte spat, rising to signal the end of the meeting.

After signing the order for Moreau's arrest, the councillors filed out, leaving Réal and Régnier with Bonaparte. 'Go and see Moreau and tell him just enough of what we've unearthed of his plot,' Bonaparte told them.

'If he wants to see me, bring him here and we'll settle this business man to man.'

Now he had persuaded the council to back him and could arrest his rival, he hesitated. Why provoke Moreau's supporters to take to the streets and foment a revolution? Why divide the army against both of them? Why arrest and probably execute one of the country's best generals? On the other hand, give Moreau room for manoeuvre and he could seize power.

Impatient for the return of Régnier and Réal, he strode up and down the long salon fronting the courtyard, inhaling pinch after pinch of snuff. Finally, when the carriage appeared, he noticed with surprise Réal had come back alone. 'Moreau's not with you, then?'

'No, Consul, he didn't even ask to see you.'

'That's what it is to deal with imbeciles,' he muttered, leaving Réal wondering if he meant Moreau or Régnier, or both. Within minutes, Réal left, carrying an order to Murat for Moreau's arrest.

'Did he put up a fight?' he asked, when both men brought news the republican general was lying in the Temple.

'He didn't even seem surprised,' Murat said.

'Did he ask to write to me?'

Réal shook his head, adding Moreau had denied or rebutted every piece of evidence connecting him with any plot by Pichegru or Cadoudal.

'All right,' Bonaparte said, glaring at them. 'Moreau doesn't know me well enough. Since he doesn't want to confess to me, he'll have to confess before a court of justice — or at the foot of the guillotine.'

8

Next morning, General Charles Pichegru became aware that every policeman and every republican soldier and sympathizer was looking for him and Cadoudal. Placarded on walls and hoardings, on public buildings and reproduced in the Press, a proclamation signed by General Joachim Murat alerted the people about the conspiracy. Judging from its style and substance, Bonaparte himself had dictated it to his brother-in-law.

It ran:

Soldiers: fifty brigands, the rotten remains of the civil war, have disembarked at night from the Beville (sic) cliffs! Georges [Cadoudal] and General Pichegru were at their head. Their arrival has been encouraged by a man who still counts in our ranks, General Moreau, who was yesterday placed in custody by the state police. The former general Lajolais is in irons; the police are on the trail of Georges [Cadoudal] and Pichegru. In these circumstances, so afflicting for the heart of the First Consul, we soldiers of the mother country shall be the first to make a shield of our bodies.

With the arrest of General Lajolais, his aide, Pichegru had lost his hideout. His friend, Xavier Janson, former Mayor of Besançon, found him lodgings with a dressmaker in the Saint-Germain district, but when this woman discovered they were hunting for him, she turned him into the street. There he wandered with nothing but his broad-brimmed hat and silk-lined cape to conceal his identity.

He might have sought refuge with the Chouans, but he would have endangered them. At any moment, he risked capture, for so many Parisians would recognize him from his famous days as saviour of the country; some might remember him as the man who had turned his guns on the *sans-culottes* when they rose in 1795 against the national convention; many would know him as the turncoat who had led the abortive royalist *coup d'état* and had landed in Devil's Island. Yet, he had nowhere else to go; he was trapped in Paris.

For weeks he flitted from one sordid hiding-place to another, from lodging-houses in the slum districts to empty basements filled with tramps and rats. He had lain low with his brother for a day before Bonaparte's police had swooped with search warrants to ransack the place then keep Abbé Pichegru under surveillance. Sometimes he patrolled the streets all night, but even then passers-by peered at his tall, loose-limbed figure enveloped in the cape and hat.

His trek through the jungles and swamps of Devil's Island and Guyana seemed much less of an ordeal than groping through this human jungle where 40,000 armed men and most of the 700,000 citizens were tracking him. On every street, on public buildings and café windows, he saw posters offering 100,000 pounds reward for information leading to his capture. Those who harboured himself, Cadoudal or anyone in the plot could be guillotined; those who met or talked to them could expect six years in irons.

Pichegru considered making for Switzerland on foot, but a sight of the guarded ramparts and gates of Paris banished that notion; bayonets and pikes probed every hay cart, and each wagon and carriage was submitted to meticulous searches on entering and leaving the capital. In the low cafés where he ate, he overheard they were even opening coffins and prying into hearses transporting the dead out of Paris for burial in the provinces.

On Sunday, 26 February, Pichegru came across a widow he had known while commanding the northern army. Remarried to a merchant called Treille, she remembered the young general who had actually paid for the merchandise delivered to his troops. She and her husband offered him food and a bed as long as he needed them, but the merchant's home, above his warehouse, proved too dangerous with the comings and goings of tradesmen and shopkeepers who might have spotted him.

Madame Treille had an idea. Why not ask Monsieur Leblanc, her husband's bachelor friend and fellow-mason to lend his lodgings for the time being? Leblanc immediately offered the general his humble room and found himself temporary lodgings. What a pleasure to help the Conqueror of Holland and Saviour of *La Patrie*! What an honour that he should place his confidence in a nondescript man like himself!

Madame Treille and her daughter accompanied both men through Paris to the grim apartment block at 39 Rue de Chabanais. In the small, second-floor room, the two ladies fixed a bed for Monsieur Prouvost, as they called him, then thanked Leblanc, saying one day France would feel grateful to him for his courage.

Left to himself, Charles Pichegru undressed, folding his clothing army-fashion. One pistol he left in a pocket, the other he thrust under his pillow; his square-bladed dagger he placed on the bedside table. Before getting into bed, he studied the door which looked so flimsy he jostled a chest of drawers against it, then, leaving his oil lamp burning he turned over to drop into a weary sleep.

A crash woke him as the door splintered; overturning the chest of drawers. Before Pichegru could recover his wits, several men sprang at him and pinioned him to the bed. Over went the bedside table, spilling the oil which blazed up to reveal half-a-dozen gendarmes round the bed.

Although dazed, Pichegru levered two men off his body and wrestled a third to the floor. Blows rained on the head and back of the fallen general as the three others leapt to aid their comrades. Yet, Pichegru, roaring like a bull and battling like a lion, picked up one man and hurled him at the others. He paused to wipe the blood from his eyes and a crack on his shin and a truncheon on his head felled him once more. But he rose again to grapple with two of his assailants, gouging and punching at the policemen who had rent his nightshirt and were trying to restrain and bind his flailing arms and legs.

Finally, one of the gendarmes ripped away his shirt, caught him by the testicles and squeezed until Pichegru bellowed with agony and writhed to the floor. Still yelling, Pichegru could do no more while they trussed him with ropes and wrapped him in a quilt. In this way, they bore him through the crowds attracted by the violence of the fight to the commissariat in Rue des Saints-Pères.

When they untied him, even François Réal let drop his official mask and shook his head in sorrow on seeing the naked giant, his body covered in bruises and contusions, his face a bloody mess. Four of the police escort needed medical attention. He gave Pichegru time to bathe his face and bruises and dress before interrogating him.

'What are you called?' he began.

'I'm called Pichegru.'

'Christian names?'

'I have one — Charles.'

'You have come here from England. Whom did you see regularly in England?'

'Everybody.'

'Didn't you see some of the French princes?'

'Yes, I saw them all.'

'Didn't you often meet the former Comte d'Artois?'

'No more often than the others.'

'Why did you leave England to come to France?'

Pichegru gazed at Réal then said, 'You know the story well enough since you remember me as president of the convention. Ten years ago, I left France through the manoeuvrings of Bonaparte who hated me because I condemned his conduct during the riots of 4 October, 1795, when he murdered true Frenchmen. Then he lent the Directory his support to crush the royalist revolt of 1797 and banish me and others to Guyana. Why have I come back? Because I was tired of living outside my own country and reading calumnies, inspired by Bonaparte, saying I was at the head of foreign armies bent on destroying France. I thought I could do no better than return. That is all I can tell you.'

Pichegru refused to answer all other questions. Cadoudal? Moreau? He had not seen Moreau since 1797 and he knew nothing of a plot between Cadoudal and Moreau apart from the rubbish imagined by Bonaparte and plastered all over Parisian walls and buildings by his lackey, Murat.

Despite himself, Réal admired the nobility and courage of this man. 'General, I implore you to tell the truth,' he said. 'A man who has commanded republican armies and filled

Europe with his exploits has no business with a gang of wild men and knaves like Chouans.'

'Don't make insinuations and put them in my mouth and accuse me of lying,' Pichegru retorted, thrusting aside the quill Réal proffered for him to sign his deposition. When they had placed him in his cell at the Temple Prison, he scrawled on the wall, 'I, Charles Pichegru, have been betrayed and sold to Bonaparte's police by the infamous Jansen, Mayor of Besançon.'

No one had told him the name of the real Judas.

Later that morning, Réal and Murat brought the First Consul news of Pichegru's arrest and the statement he had made. It landed on the carpet for Méneval to retrieve.

'So, he'll only talk in front of a judge in a court of law,' he muttered. Pichegru obviously had revelations to make, and he racked his mind wondering what sort. 'Keep at him,' he said. 'But no torture.' He stabbed a finger at Réal. 'And remember, I want a report of everything he says. Everything.'

'What do we do about this little runt, Leblanc?' Murat asked. He related how Leblanc had come to disclose he had installed the general in his own room. 'He even drew me a sketch and gave me two keys to earn his bounty.'

'Evidently a very conscientious citizen,' Bonaparte said, drily.

'I'd like to put him against a wall.'

'No, we have to pay him his 100,000 pounds. But frighten him away from Paris and order him to say nothing to anyone.'

'And Pichegru?' Réal queried. 'What line do I take with him?'

'Find out what sort of defence he might put forward,' Bonaparte replied, and the councillor noticed that twitching right shoulder, a sign something was nagging the consul's mind. 'Confine your questions and your depositions to the conspiracy, but note privately anything else he says and report it to me.'

'And if he won't talk . . . ?'

'I said, no torture.' Bonaparte went to gaze through a window at the courtyard. 'I knew General Pichegru at Brienne when I was a boy who could hardly speak French and they called me 'the Italian' and joked about my name, Napoleone. Pichegru never treated me with anything but respect and kindness. He is also a great soldier and a brave man who has made a mistake.'

'We won't need his confession when we capture Cadoudal,' Murat put in.

'First you have to capture him,' Bonaparte retorted, rounding on his brother-in-law.

'What dispositions have you made?'

Murat outlined how he had strengthened the guards on all entry points and customs posts; his men were searching every building that had ever harboured Chouans and were sifting the Saint-Germain district house by house for secret hiding places; he had also posted Cadoudal's description on a thousand walls and had raised the rewards to 250,000 pounds.

'You've forgotten the barges and river traffic. Search that, too.'

Bonaparte crossed the room and seized a list from Méneval's files. 'These are the forty-odd Chouan leaders named and described by the prisoners. Copy them and post them everywhere, and see that nobody enters or leaves the capital without written authorization from the police prefect.'

He looked at Murat, then at Réal. 'You know, a whole army hunted Cadoudal for two years and he made a fool of everybody. Now that we've trapped him in Paris we must catch him and nail the conspiracy.'

9

After shutting the Chaillot mansion, Cadoudal went to a new hideout above a fruit shop in Rue Montagne-Sainte-Genevieve. A young woman called Marie-Madeleine Hisay found it for him. She had acted as a Chouan courier recruited by Hozier, who considered her more royalist than Cadoudal himself. Ugly, ill-dressed, walking with a congenital limp, she seemed the antithesis of any sort of plotter. A talisman protected her, a medallion containing part of the True Cross and Christ's crown of thorns. Neither the grocer, Madame Lemoine, nor her daughter could conceive of such a girl lying when she explained Monsieur Soudan (Cadoudal) and his companion Aimé Joyaux were in hiding after killing someone in a duel.

Both Chouans sensed the net was tightening round them. 'Why don't we make for Brittany and lie low there until the hunt has died down?' Joyaux suggested.

'And leave the men who trusted us and followed us here to pay for our folly with their lives? No, we stay and take our chance.'

'It only needs one of them to talk.'

'They still have to find us.'

Now, wherever Cadoudal went, he risked capture. Throughout the capital, he noticed knots of people studying his description or having it read to them. With their new proclamation, Bonaparte's police had excelled themselves, giving his age (33), his height and other measurements to the millimetre, his hairstyle, his accent and details he himself had hardly spotted.

Did he swagger and turn his palms outwards? Did he have a double chin? A kink in his nose? Why, they even mentioned he could not stand tobacco smoke. For all their descriptive prose, he moved through Paris, rubbing shoulders with police and soldiers in daylight and darkness for weeks without once incurring suspicion.

Parisian stories amused him. Georges had already escaped in a coffin after body-snatching its occupant; Georges had quietly swum down the Seine past the customs house and was now in Brittany; Georges had merely walked through the Porte d'Auteuil disguised as one of Bonaparte's ADCs.

And so on. He might have done any of these things and quit the capital. Aimé Joyaux had even suggested mustering their faithful and fighting a pitched battle with the republican guards while Cadoudal slipped through a gate. This and other escape methods he waved aside. He would stay to the end.

Yet, he realized his vital strike had failed, nothing detained him in Paris. One by one, he saw a dozen others follow the two generals into the Temple Prison. When they arrested both the Polignac princes, then the Marquis de Rivière, he felt guilty of betraying the Bourbon cause.

Although he disguised himself and took no risks, he had several narrow escapes. One night, two of Réal's policemen followed him into a cul-de-sac in the Saint-Denis suburb. With no chance of flight, he armed his two pistols and was turning to face the detectives when he caught sight of a plaque inscribed, Monsieur Guilbert, Dental Surgeon. A girl answered his knock and he pushed into the house.

'But my master's asleep at this hour,' the girl protested.

'I'm in agony, go and wake him,' Cadoudal said, clutching his jaw.

In dressing-gown, Monsieur Guilbert hurried through to find a huge figure draped in a white smock already in his dental chair. 'That one,' he said pointing to a back molar.

'Nothing wrong with it I can see.'

'Well, I can feel it. Take it out'

Guilbert went to object when he spotted two pistols protruding from his patient's waistband. Hands shaking, he locked his forceps round the healthy tooth and wrenched it out. Two things struck him: his patient took an inordinate time rinsing his mouth, and two strangers chose that moment to peer through his window then disappear. Yet, the man paid him handsomely and thanked him profusely.

After that scare, Cadoudal decided to find a safer house and separate from Joyaux. But where? Charles d'Hozier offered his own hideout with a second-hand-clothes dealer, but he refused. Finally Aimé Joyaux discovered the best cache in Paris, made by the master hand of Spain himself. In Rue du Four at la Reine des Fleurs, a perfumery run by Antoine Caron, a royalist sympathizer. Above its broad window, the signboard jutted over the street. Behind this, Spain had fashioned a hollow compartment which would accommodate one man crouching or lying flat. Guillaume Hyde de Neuville and other famous royalists had used Caron's house and cache. But at first, the perfumier hesitated, aware of the huge manhunt for Cadoudal and the danger he himself ran. Eventually, he said yes.

By now it was impossible for Cadoudal to

move even the mile between the two hideouts without an elaborate plan. He detailed his aide, Louis Le Ridant to hire a cabriolet for the whole of 9 March, hide it until darkness then pick him up at the top of Montagne-Sainte-Genevieve.

Aimé Joyaux took his life in his hands to cross Paris and settle the arrangements with Le Ridant at his lodgings. He failed to notice the young Breton student who had a shakedown bed in Le Ridant's entrance. This youth, named Gougeon, overheard the conversation and hurried to the police prefecture to return with a reward of 2,000 francs in his pocket. Next morning, making an excuse, he persuaded Le Ridant to lend him the cabriolet. At the police headquarters they recorded its number — 53 — and a description of the driver so they could track its progress through Paris.

Just before seven, Cadoudal donned his favourite disguise, the overalls, boots and broad-brimmed felt cap of a Paris market porter. Quitting his room, he walked up Rue Montagne-Sainte-Genevieve to the rendezvous. For several minutes, he waited in a doorway until he recognized Le Ridant in the driver's seat of an approaching cabriolet. But, as the vehicle slowed and he hoisted up his bulky figure beside the aide, someone cried, 'Stop thief!'

It seemed a small army of police

materialized in the lamplight round the cab. Joyaux and two other Chouans, who had scouted the mute, drove at the detectives with their knives. 'The whip,' Cadoudal shouted and Le Ridant thrashed the tired nag into a gallop. Coming under the dark mass of the Pantheon, Cadoudal turned to see three policemen gaining on the cab. One ran past and threw himself at the horse's head. Cadoudal fired one of his pistols, hitting the policeman on the temple, killing him instantly. At that moment, the old horse gave up and both Cadoudal and Le Ridant jumped to the ground and began running.

As he ducked into the Rue de l'Observance, Cadoudal heard someone behind him. He turned as the man charged at him, long baton raised to strike. Cocking his second pistol, he fired. Too soon. His ball grazed the policeman's left shoulder and he rushed on, bringing his stave down on Cadoudal's head. Although dazed, Cadoudal felled the man with a blow, rounded and ran down the steps. Fifty yards on, he began to walk, calmly. Only 300 strides lay between him and safety.

But now the whole district had filled with policemen. His pursuers had found the empty cab, the dead policeman. Like so many sharks, they were following the bloody trail left by their wounded comrade, Inspector

Caillole. Heads were appearing at every window and street crowds were collecting. To deflect their attention, Cadoudal placed himself in a conspicuous position, under a lamp-post outside the lottery ticket office; there, his floppy, broad-brimmed porter's cap shaded his face and would, he hoped, enable him to pass undetected.

But a policeman spotted him and cried, 'Over here, comrades, it's him.'

Cadoudal might have pulled out his dagger, struck the man down and made another bolt for it. But he had run far enough. It seemed he had spent most of his short life flitting from one hiding-place to another. Anyway, sooner or later they would arrest him. No more than he deserved. His mission had ended in disaster and all those promises to the Bourbon princes and English statesmen had gone unfulfilled.

Most of the small band he had brought here with such high hopes were resisting daily torture because they refused to reveal his whereabouts. Now they would suffer no longer. Moreover, he had become a dead weight for brave men like Joyaux and Hozier, who might now slip through the Paris cordon to safety in the provinces.

'It's him, it's Georges.'

'Yes, it's me — Georges Cadoudal.'

Policemen and passers-by surrounded him. Caillole, the wounded inspector, dragged himself down the steps to produce the rope and bind him. He submitted quietly, letting them tie his hands and arms behind his back and thrust him into a police van which took him to the prefecture on the Quai des Orfevres.

* * *

In the prefect's office, he recognized Réal and a hatchet-faced man who had become a by-word for blood-soiled revolutionaries — Jacques-Alexis Thuriot, friend then enemy of Robespierre and prime mover in the execution of Louis XVI. He fixed Cadoudal with bloodshot eyes that seemed to weep permanently. Two other men identified themselves as Dubois, the police prefect, and Desmarest, chief of the secret police. They flung question after question, accusation after accusation at him, but alone in his many caches he had so often rehearsed this scene that he knew how to disarm his interrogators.

'I am Georges Cadoudal, aged thirty-three, native of Brech near Auray in Morbihan Department, a soldier by profession without domicile in Paris,' he answered without prompting.

225

'What did you come to Paris for?'

'I came to attack the First Consul,' Cadoudal replied, and watched amazement and consternation on the four faces.

'What were your means of attacking the First Consul?'

'I had few means. I was counting on assembling them.'

'You live at Chaillot.'

'I shall not say where I live.'

'Do you know Pichegru?'

'I met him in London.'

'You saw him in Paris. You were together at Chaillot, we know that.'

'I have already replied I had no lodgings in Paris.'

'What was the nature of your means to attack the First Consul?'

'Force.'

'Did you have many men with you?'

'No, I had to attack the First Consul only when there was a prince in Paris. He is not yet here.'

He denied ordering the Saint-Nicaise attempt on Bonaparte's life. 'I told Saint-Réjant to prepare the means of attack but not to carry out the coup of Christmas Eve 1800.'

To try to break Cadoudal's resolve, Thuriot had policemen bring in the body of the gendarme he had shot. 'You killed the father of a family,' he snapped.

'You should have had me arrested by bachelors.'

'What were you doing with the portrait of the former Louis XVI which was found in your possession?'

Cadoudal faced him out. 'And you, Tue-Roi[1] what did you do with the original?'

'What was your project?'

'To replace Bonaparte with a Bourbon.'

'Which Bourbon was chosen?'

'Chosen!' Cadoudal flinched at this term, then declared, 'Louis Xavier-Stanislas, recognized by us as Louis XVIII.'

'What role were you to play during the attack?'

'The role the French prince in Paris assigned me.'

'So, the plan had been conceived and had to be executed in association with the former French princes?' Cadoudal nodded. 'Was Pichegru part of this conspiracy?'

'I don't know.'

'Moreau, was he one of you?'

'I have neither seen nor know him.'

Thuriot brandished the dagger found on Cadoudal when arrested, the one Captain John Wright had given him. 'Wasn't this

---

[1] Literally, king-killer.

227

dagger made in England?'

'Yes, citizen.'

'Therefore controlled by the English?'

'No.'

'Rather than attack with force, wasn't it with a dagger like this, supported by your gang, that you were going to assassinate the First Consul?'

'I was going to attack with the same weapons his escort and guard carried.'

'In England were you at the head of an army corps paid by the English treasury.'

'No. Several officers I commanded in the west went to England, but they were not employed, no more than I was, myself.'

At that, Cadoudal shut his mouth, refusing to answer further questions. For ten hours without a break they had questioned him. Now, they escorted him under a cavalry detachment to the tower of the Temple Prison.

In an adjoining cell, lay General Pichegru whom he could just perceive when they opened both doors. Enough to gesture to each other they had divulged nothing of the real conspiracy. In another cell sat Bouvet de Lozier, immured in self-reproach for having betrayed them in his hour of cowardice. Cadoudal managed to signal that he had forgiven him, but he should say nothing more.

As for himself, he stretched on the low, wooden bed and closed his mouth and eyes to both guards and interrogators and remained immobile, as though he had already shut out the world.

10

At the Tuileries, Réal learned the First Consul
was spending several days at Malmaison,
which he often did at the beginning of spring.
Driving through the grounds, his eye dwelt
with pleasure on the exotic plants Joséphine
had imported from her native Caribbean
island, and the gardens she had designed all
round the long, low mansion and its artificial
lake. Turning at the rose garden, his carriage
almost collided with another leaving the
house. A pair of hooded eyelids blinked in
wintry acknowledgement from its interior.
Talleyrand! What skulduggery had that
aristocrat from Perigord been whispering to
his master? His presence acted on Réal like a
cloud over the sun.

Behind the mansion, Réal's astonished gaze
met a striped campaign tent pitched between
the study and the bridge leading to the
croquet lawns. Inside, Bonaparte had smoth-
ered two folding tables with maps and was
dictating to Méneval who sat writing with
cramped fingers, his bleak face regretting his
warm billet at the Tuileries. Glancing at the
maps of Europe and Asia Minor, the state

councillor for security asked himself what other worlds Bonaparte was now aiming to conquer.

'Ah, Réal,' Bonaparte cried, drawing a deep breath and exhaling. 'Fresh air and a sight of the sky, that's what gives me inspiration. I don't know how people can work cooped up in offices and houses all day.'

Seizing the papers Réal proffered, he scanned them, his eyes backtracking from time to time with a query in them. 'Well,' he said, finally, 'Cadoudal seems to have told us most of what we needed to know.'

Réal nodded, though remarking he had also protected Pichegru and Moreau.

'No matter,' Bonaparte said. He could not help admitting to himself Cadoudal had behaved with much more credit and dignity than the men who had interrogated him. This Chouan leader meant to assume all the responsibility, thus exonerating all the other leaders. As he re-read the document his eye halted several times at the phrase: 'No, I had to attack the First Consul only when there was a prince in Paris . . . '

Réal noticed Bonaparte was taking pinch after pinch of snuff from an empty box before he muttered, 'Cadoudal didn't say anything else about this prince, did he?'

Réal shook his head then fished another

sheaf of papers out of his file. 'But his driver, le Ridant, said he had seen this prince.'

'Let me have that.' Bonaparte grabbed the papers and sat down to study them. Asked about a prince, le Ridant replied he had often heard Cadoudal speak of this prince. Then he observed a young man of about twenty-five appear at Chaillot who had distinguished manners and whom everyone treated like a prince. Bonaparte recalled Querelle's evidence about someone coming from England, but Savary had assured him no one could have landed from that side. Picot had described a man in an elegant cape who had given Cadoudal orders.

Where had this prince appeared from? Ever since his disappointment over the Biville expedition, Bonaparte had longed to get his hands on a Bourbon prince. Any prince. He would settle scores with those blue-bloods who thought they could send their thugs and cut-throats to murder him. As an army commander, he had always struck at the head, and he would deal himself with these aristocrats who had armed the hands of these Chouans and royalists. An eye for an eye. Who could blame him for acting in self-defence? If he caught one of the Bourbon princes and put him against a wall, it would solve many of his political problems: for one thing, he would convince diehard Jacobins like Fouché and so many others he had no intention of restoring the monarchy and putting their lives in jeopardy; secondly, he would prove to royalists like this fanatic, Cadoudal, that their cause had no future; thirdly, and most important for Bonaparte, he could found a new dynasty — his own — on the blood of a Bourbon and the trial and execution of these plotters.

All France would tremble at how close these royalist conspirators had come to leaving her without Bonaparte to govern and win her glory. He would have no difficulty persuading the French people they needed not a first consul for life, but a dynasty beginning with Napoleon the First.

Talleyrand, who had just left him, used similar arguments about the princes' conspiracy. 'If justice forces us to punish, politics forces us to punish without exception,' the old fox had said. A good maxim. Then Talleyrand, the man who had weathered every political and social tempest during the revolution, spelled it out for him. 'You can only have one aim, sire, stabilize the government and assure the people's security. To do this you have only one means — you must appoint your successor.'

'How?' Bonaparte asked, though aware of the answer.

'You need a head, sire.'

'A head?'

'A noble head,' Talleyrand specified. 'The revolution needed the head of Louis XVI to keep the Bourbons running. You need another one to prevent their return.'

Not for the first time did Bonaparte find himself thinking like this old sophist. He had reasoned in exactly the same way when he sent Savary to the coast to capture Artois or Berri. But Talleyrand had given him another name. Louis Antoine Henri de Bourbon Condé, Duc d'Enghien. Of all the Bourbons only he had the courage and will to attempt a *coup d'état*.

Didn't he live just across the Rhine at Ettenheim, within half-an-hour's march of French soil, waiting to strike? Hadn't he already led part of the army of his grandfather, the Prince of Condé, against the French, and not without success? And, as the First Consul was aware, intelligence agents in London talked of how he was slipping in and out of Strasbourg and even venturing as far as Paris. All Talleyrand's arguments had sounded rational, although Bonaparte did not need persuading. Artois, Berri, Enghien — what did it matter which royal prince, if he served the right purpose?

Réal interrupted his musings by proffering

a silver snuffbox which Bonaparte grabbed, used, then shoved into his waistcoat pocket. How many boxes had the policeman seen disappear in that way? Bonaparte turned to him. 'Well, Réal, I think the most vital part of this testimony is what Cadoudal and his men say about the prince. Have you started these checks on Enghien?'

Réal nodded. Two of their spies had crossed the Rhine. One of them had discovered Enghien had just received two newcomers from England. 'The first man's an English diplomat called Smith, but you'd never guess who the other is — Dumouriez.'

'Dumouriez!' Bonaparte literally bounded at the name. As a republican general, Charles François Dumouriez had achieved as much as Pichegru, conquering Belgium and winning his battles brilliantly. Then he went over to the royalists and wound up in England.

'That renegade. Is he now in the plot with Pichegru and Moreau and this royal duke?'

'Our evidence points that way.'

'Then you and Régnier must confirm it and bring me the proof. A prince ten miles from my frontier organizing my murder!'

So incensed did he seem that he offered his state councillor snuff from the box he had stolen, then thrust it back into his pocket and dismissed Réal.

★ ★ ★

Day by day, evidence built up against Enghien who seemed the natural leader of the conspiracy and the *coup d'état*. In the past, his grandfather, Condé, had intrigued with Pichegru; and the young duke, last of his line, had fought valiantly with the Duke of Brunswick in his abortive attempt to restore the monarchy and had covered himself with glory in several battles against republican armies.

Such a man might win over those royalists who felt Louis XVIII and his brother, Artois, lacked the qualities of kingship; they might even promote Enghien from tenth to first in the line for the restored monarchy. So ran the convenient and self-fulfilling argument with which Bonaparte convinced himself.

Reports began to filter back from his London and Rhineland spies informing him Enghien had offered his services to England through Sir Charles Stuart, the British ambassador in Vienna; he was receiving £250 a month, the pay of a retired general; he had a staff of five or six officers; he had always advocated raising an army to invade France, picking up support in Alsace, Provence, the western provinces and overthrowing the government.

To clinch all this reasoning, they had the description of the young prince who had visited Cadoudal at Chaillot. Tall, elegant, handsome, aged about twenty-five: it fitted Enghien. No one thought of comparing that portrait with young Jules de Polignac, who lay in a cell not twenty yards from Cadoudal; no one thought of confronting him with the arrested Chouans who had mistaken him for the royal prince who was coming to lead their coup.

'Make a secret reconnaissance of Enghien's house, the area around it and his movements,' Bonaparte ordered Réal. This told him Enghien lived a simple life in a mansion outside Ettenheim in the Electorate of Bade with his mistress, Charlotte de Rohan-Rochefort, an elegant and beautiful princess who had followed him into exile. Friends whispered they had married secretly in defiance of his father's opposition to the liaison.

German villagers watched them walk hand-in-hand on their small estate or potter in their flower and vegetable garden; they also met Enghien in the forests along the Rhine banks with his two hunting dogs and a shotgun over his arm. They knew him for a patriot who would stand for hours gazing across the Rhine at Alsace and the fudged imprint of the Vosges Mountains, homesick for his own country.

No one guarded the house, the spies reported, and, as far as they knew, Enghien kept to his side of the Rhine.

Reading these accounts, Bonaparte reflected he might have to wait years to catch the duke on French soil. However, he decided he had enough evidence to act there and then. Méneval entered his study one evening to find it covered with maps and charts of the Rhineland between Strasbourg and Freiburg. Plying a ruler and compasses, Bonaparte was calculating routes and distances between German and Alsatian towns and between Alsace and Paris.

'Méneval, I'm calling a special council meeting. Same letter and same people as for the meeting on Moreau.'

This time, however, not all the council sided with him, or agreed his police and spies had proved Enghien's guilt. Talleyrand voted for the arrest and trial; so did Fouché, who hated the Bourbons; Chief Justice Régnier and Réal had collected the evidence and could do no more than cast their options with the First Consul's. But both the other consuls stood out against the summary trial and execution of a Bourbon duke who was living as an exile in another country. Lebrun, royalist by temperament, said that to abduct Enghien would cause a diplomatic row in Europe and set every hand against France. Cambacérès went even further. Agreed, he had voted the death of Louis XVI, but he had also urged a pardon for the condemned king. Even if guilty, which he doubted, the duke's life should be spared.

Bonaparte listened, flint-eyed, waiting for the right moment to lose his temper. He shouted at Cambacérès, 'The Bourbons think they can spill my blood like killing vermin. My blood's as good as theirs. I shall have the first of these princes who falls into my hands shot without mercy.'

'Surely you wouldn't go that far,' Cambacérès came back.

Bonaparte glared at him. 'You've become very thrifty with Bourbon blood,' he retorted.

Cambacérès listened in silence as the First Consul and others discussed the arrest and abduction of the Duc d'Enghien. When they had finished, he appealed once more to Bonaparte for clemency. 'My dear General,' he said, 'up to now you have been fortunate to remain a stranger to the crimes of the Revolution, but if you soil your hands with Bourbon blood, you will be associated with those crimes as well. Spare yourself regrets like mine.'

Bonaparte shook his head. 'This is the seventh major conspiracy against me in my three years in office and I cannot count the assassination attempts I have foiled. This time it's not only my existence that is threatened, but that of France herself. She is threatened with foreign invaders and a civil war. It must cease and it will cease only when I strike at the root cause. Justice will be done.' He refused to listen to both consuls and closed the debate.

Watching them filter silently away, he wondered which of them knew his real purpose in arresting and trying Enghien. Perhaps none, except Talleyrand and Fouché. For the others he remained the jumped-up general who would have his run of power and retire. A general might know where to start a campaign like this one, but it took a statesman to predict where it would finish. He had done that throughout his tussle with the conspirators.

To the one person whom he should have informed, in whom he normally confided everything, he said nothing. For a long time he deliberated whether to tell Joséphine and decided against it. He could predict her reaction. She would implore him not to commit this crime. So, it was better to face her with a *fait accompli*.

11

Alone in his tent at Malmaison, he prepared the raid on the mansion across the Rhine as meticulously as he had planned the crossing of the Alps. Nothing must go amiss. Two companies of 200 and 300 cavalry would ford the Rhinau ferry in the early hours of 15 March.

Before dawn, one company under General Michel Ordener would swoop on Enghien and his staff while the other, under his aide, the Marquis de Caulaincourt, would round up the pocket of royalists and British agents his spies had uncovered further north at Offenburg. With a six-horse team changed every twenty miles, they could lodge their prisoner in the Château de Vincennes inside three days.

Everything went as planned. At five o'clock, Ordener and Caulaincourt struck. Not even a shot halted them at Enghien's country house; the young duke had the choice of fighting or fleeing, but to spare his staff and the woman he loved, he did neither, submitting quietly. Dressing in his hunting clothes, he kissed Princess Charlotte goodbye then mounted and accompanied the cavalry to the Rhine which they forded.

No one had told Enghien why they had taken him prisoner, why they were leading him back into France. Once on Alsatian soil they placed him under guard in a berlin coach and set off for Strasbourg. As they jogged along, something clawed through the open window of the carriage and landed at the duke's feet. Mohilof the elder of his two black-and-tan foxhounds, lay exhausted at his feet, its tongue lolling, its body dripping wet. He had swum the broad River Rhine to follow his master into captivity.

But in Paris, Bonaparte realized things had begun to go awry. No one around Ettenheim had ever encountered Dumouriez; they had confused him with Enghien's friend, the harmless Marquis de Thumery. And the English diplomat, Smith, had become Schmidt, a German subject. At Offenburg, the expected royalist rebels and British spies did not materialize.

To compound the mystery, Enghien denied all collusion with the French renegade general or English diplomats and spies when interrogated at Strasbourg. Then, as the convoy headed for Paris at full gallop, a courier brought Bonaparte papers they had seized at Ettenheim, which gave no hint of a conspiracy or a *coup d'état*. With them came a letter from Enghien refuting allegations that he had taken part in the Cadoudal plot.

Ignoring the evidence and brushing aside every objection, Bonaparte made preparations for the trial. Before the duke had arrived, he was drafting a list of eight officers for the military tribunal, which would sentence the last of the royal line of Condé. At their head he placed General Pierre Hulin, a dedicated Jacobin who had helped storm the Bastille then rose through the revolutionary ranks to become a general. Bonaparte had even drawn up a list of questions to put to Enghien. Summoning Réal, he handed him both lists with instructions to interrogate Enghien before the trial.

'So you're not going to put him on public trial, Consul?'

'No question of that,' Bonaparte barked. 'He'll be tried like a traitor caught with arms in his hand on French soil.'

When Réal objected they had arrested him in a foreign country and had no proof he was a traitor, Bonaparte glared at him, waved him out of the study and turned his back.

By this time, Joséphine had got wind of Enghien's arrest and came to plead for his release. 'Women should keep out of these affairs,' he growled at her.

'All right, Bonaparte. But if you let them judge and execute your prisoner you'll be guillotined yourself like my first husband. And this time I shall keep you company.'

His laugh followed her out of the study. From the window of her upstairs apartments at Malmaison, she and Hortense watched the ministers come and go; Bonaparte strolled with them around her botanic gardens and rose beds, well out of earshot of anyone, to discuss the Enghien case. Fouché, she knew, would advocate summary trial and death, but he had ceased to influence Bonaparte.

When they saw Talleyrand bending his game leg to whisper something in his master's ear, Hortense turned to her mother. 'That limping man makes me feel sick,' she said. Murat, Réal, Régnier — they all had their half-hour in the gardens. Then another man whom Joséphine disliked, despised and distrusted: General René Savary. Like a morgue-keeper or an undertaker, he stank of death.

On 20 March, when he had conferred with all the other ministers, Bonaparte summoned Savary to give him his orders and a letter for Murat. 'You understand,' he told Savary, 'everything must be finished tonight and the sentence, of which there can be no doubt, is to be put into effect immediately.' Savary nodded. On this occasion he not only looked like the First Consul, he could almost feel his master's thoughts and emotions. They were both getting their revenge for the abortive Biville expedition.

★ ★ ★

When the carriage finally stopped, the Duc d'Enghien recognized the Château de Vincennes with its rectangular fortress hemmed in by a dry moat; not long before the Revolution, he had come there as a child. Now he sat down in a bare cell to the frugal meal of cold meat and noodles which the gaoler's wife had prepared. Although he had eaten nothing all day and was starving, he fed Mohilof half his food, watching the dog's dark eyes searching his face for some explanation. Enghien could not enlighten him, for no one had officially mentioned the reason for his arrest. Whatever it was, they would surely give him a fair trial. At the most, he could expect a long period of detention.

Just before eleven that night, two guards roused him and escorted him before a military tribunal. Enghien had no defence lawyer and knew neither the general nor the five colonels and two majors who sat on the bench; another stranger — Savary

— stood spectating at this scene, as silent as Mohilof. When General Hulin read the charge, Enghien realized a summary court-martial in the field would have given him a fairer trial, and these men meant to sentence him to death.

First, they charged him as an *émigré* prince with having been caught on the French frontier, arms in hand. Then came the questions, all of them phrased in such a way he could not deny them completely. Have you borne arms against France? Have you been in the pay of the English? Have you wished to offer your services to England to fight against the republic? Have you not contacted the English to offer your services to lead an expedition into France?

Enghien's honesty forced him to answer these questions with a qualified Yes. But he rebutted any notion that he had associated with General Dumouriez, Pichegru, Moreau or Cadoudal; he repeated he remained ignorant of Cadoudal and his conspiracy; he had never visited Strasbourg let alone made secret visits to Paris. If and when he decided to come to Paris he would not keep such a visit secret, he said.

'I have done no more than sustain the rights of my family,' he insisted.

'And if the opportunity presented itself

again, would you take up arms against France?' General Hulin asked.

'A Condé can never enter France without arms in his hands,' the duke replied. 'My birth and my opinions must always make me inflexible on that point.'

Time and again, the tribunal put the same question, but always the duke gave the same response; he stated he would be committing no crime since he had neither sworn nor owed allegiance to the existing French Government.

When they had finished their interrogation, the judges deliberated then pronounced Enghien guilty of capital crimes; of having fought against the republic; of intriguing with the English; of having the intention of seizing the town of Strasbourg; of conspiring against the person of the First Consul.

Tired and bewildered, Enghien listened, almost refusing to believe eight Frenchmen could call what had happened a trial.

'But I'm innocent,' he protested. 'I wish to see the First Consul. I'm sure a quarter of an hour with him will clear up the confusion.'

They led him out while Hulin and his colleagues deliberated. Several of the others acceded to the prince's demand; they should allow his appeal to Bonaparte. At that moment, Savary broke his silence, stepping forward and shaking his head. 'Gentlemen,' he said, 'the First Consul has left this matter to you senior officers. I know any appeal to his personal judgment would displease him.'

'But the judgment still cannot be executed without the word of the First Consul, or the sanction of the military governor of Paris, General Murat,' Hulin objected. Calling for pen and paper, he sat down to write to Bonaparte. Savary grabbed the quill and paper from his hands.

'Your role is finished,' he shouted, then called on his gendarmes to march in the prisoner and ordered Hulin to pronounce the sentence of death while the tribunal looked on, shocked.

Enghien took the sentence calmly. 'I should like a priest to confess me,' he said.

'Why, would you die like a monk'?' Savary sneered, refusing the request.

Enghien knelt for a few moments in prayer then rose, saying, 'Let us go.'

It was three o'clock in the morning. Inside or outside the fortress, ringed with Savary's gendarmes, no one stirred. Mohilof trotted behind his master, who was still clad in his dishevelled hunting jacket, breeches and calf-boots. They pushed him down the steps to the dry moat.

There, in the lantern light, he saw they had

already dug his grave in a spot where they threw the ordure and sewage from the castle barracks. Two gendarmes positioned themselves a few yards away on either side of the duke as the officer in charge of the firing squad thrust him against the moat wall. Enghien shook his head as the man offered to bind his eyes. On the duke's left shoulder, the officer hung a lantern to show his men where to aim. At their feet, Mohilof stood, looking up at his master, puzzled.

'Have you any last wishes?' the officer whispered.

'Only for a priest.'

'No priest,' Savary shouted from the battlements where he was observing the execution.

Enghien then asked for a knife with which he cut a lock of his blond hair; from the pocket of his red hunting jacket he drew out the letter he had written while waiting to be sentenced; into the envelope he pushed the lock of hair, handing it to the officer, asking him to see that the Princess Charlotte de Rohan-Rochefort received it. When he had resumed his stance, he chased off Mohilof ordering the hound to sit outside the firing line. He nodded to the officer, then said loudly enough for everyone to hear, 'How cruel it is to die at the hands of Frenchmen.'

At a sign from Savary, the officer ordered his platoon to take aim, then shouted, 'Fire.'

Enghien pitched facedown in the mud and broken lantern glass. They had to restrain the dog from attacking while the officer put the pistol to the fallen man's temple and fired twice. His gendarmes emptied the duke's pockets before dragging him to the noisome hole into which they heaved him, without ceremony and fully-clothed.

They shovelled earth over him then left the last survivor of the great House of Condé with no one to mourn him but a demented hound which kept baying so long and so pathetically that finally one of the gaolers came down to end its grief by its master's grave with a pistol ball.

★　★　★

Talleyrand had spent a quiet evening with the Duchess de Luynes playing whist. As the Louis XVI alabaster clock on the mantelpiece chimed twice for half-past two, he threw down his cards. 'The last of the Condés is dead,' he murmured. Everyone round the table gazed at his impassive mask in horror.

At Malmaison, Bonaparte was behaving curiously. First, his brother Joseph had come with Cambacérès to plead for the young prince; his sister, Caroline, wife of Murat, begged him with tears in her eyes to spare the duke; Joséphine and Hortense had joined these and others to ask for mercy.

Bonaparte swept aside their pleas with angry comments and sat throughout dinner with a bleak face. 'Why aren't you wearing rouge?' he asked Claire de Rémusat. 'You're too pale.' He laughed. 'There are two things that suit women well — rouge and tears.'

He invited her to play chess then pushed pawns and pieces around like some novice and appeared twitchy and uneasy. When he started humming an air from a popular operetta everyone fancied that perhaps he had been play-acting and had already spared the duke's life. But he said nothing and when he had finished the game, he took Joséphine's arm and they both retired.

Next morning, Savary came to report the deed accomplished and spelled out the details. For the benefit of Méneval and his valet, Bonaparte growled they had acted too quickly; he had sent a message to Réal saying the prisoner had arrived and reminding him to go and interrogate him. Why had this not been done? Savary replied Réal had never appeared at Vincennes and they knew nothing of the Consul's message.

Summoned to Malmaison, Réal pleaded

they had given him the message only that morning. Someone had brought it after he had gone to bed, but with no instructions to wake him. Bonaparte grunted something unintelligible about the idiots around him. Réal did not take this too much to heart. By now, he knew many of his master's tricks and realized Bonaparte was merely covering his own iniquity.

Réal had only to learn of Savary's part in the legal murder of the Duc d'Enghien to assure himself that no one and nothing could have saved the victim. Savary was the Consul's hired killer. Although Savary had been at Biville when Bouvet de Lozier was arrested, Réal smelled his evil hand behind that of the gaoler, Savart, and his method of persuading Bouvet to talk. He had not forgotten that common talk linked Savary with the mysterious death of Toussaint Louverture, the Negro who had raised a black army and taken over Saint-Domingo calling himself the Bonaparte of Saint-Domingo. Brought to France after being defeated in 1802, he had lain in a dungeon at Joux Prison near Besançon where they said Savary had quietly arranged to have him garrotted. No, he could not chide himself for Enghien's death. Not when professional assassins like Savary had undertaken the task.

That day's issue of the official *Le Moniteur* stated bluntly Enghien had been both a culprit and accomplice in the conspiracy created by the English against the Consul's life. A military commission had unanimously condemned to death the said Louis Antoine Henri de Bourbon, Duc d'Enghien, for the crimes of espionage and co-operation with the enemies of the republic and attempts on the interior and exterior security of the state.

Bonaparte knew he had committed judicial murder. Even had Enghien's arrest conformed with the law, the crimes with which he had been charged lay outside the scope of a court-martial. French law also forbade midnight trials and stipulated every accused should have a defence lawyer. Only to intimate friends did Bonaparte admit the truth about Enghien's murder.

'It was a sacrifice to my grandeur and security,' he said.

Yet, it niggled at his own conscience. In Saint-Cloud stood a bust of Enghien's illustrious ancestor, the Great Condé, who had fought so valiantly and brilliantly for France in the seventeenth century. 'Take that and put it elsewhere . . . anywhere,' he told the major-domo soon after Enghien's death.

12

Of the forty-odd conspirators lying in the Temple prison, only three interested Bonaparte: the two republican generals and the one royalist. General Jean-Victor Moreau had at last condescended to write personally to him disclaiming knowledge of Pichegru and the plot, so the First Consul did not fear trouble from him when the trial took place. Cadoudal, for his part, had never done anything to deny his purpose to kill him, destroy the republic and replace its rulers with the Bourbons; he, too, would give the court nothing to worry about.

But Pichegru! For weeks he had refused to say anything to his inquisitors, stressing again and again he had revelations to make, but only to the court and the public. 'Drop everything else and keep pressing him to find out what he means,' Bonaparte instructed Réal, who wondered what was worrying the Consul so much.

Pichegru lay in one of the three top-security cells of the Temple tower; in the other two sat Cadoudal and Bouvet, both manacled, under the gaze of two goalers. No one, without the authority of Réal or Savary, could penetrate those cells, which were furnished with a bed, table and three chairs. All the other prisoners had a certain degree of liberty.

If Pichegru stonewalled against the tirades of Thuriot and the wheedlings and veiled threats of Chief-Justice Régnier, he dropped his guard somewhat with Réal as they chatted about their favourite Greek and Latin poets — from Homer and Thucidydes to Horace and Seneca.

'So, you admire Seneca,' Réal murmured.

'Yes,' Pichegru replied. 'The man Nero forced to commit suicide.'

That set Réal wondering if the general was referring to Bouvet's mysterious strangulation, or talking about himself; for the prison authorities had imagined Pichegru might take his life in the first weeks of captivity and had guarded him night and day, and still watched him more closely than the others.

Into their literary talk, Pichegru let fall several insinuations which Réal garnered, though he did nothing to prompt or cross-examine the general. Physically and intellectually, he found Pichegru no ordinary man, and he had always admired his courage and integrity. Besides winning brilliant victories in the field, he had presided over the

Five Hundred, the legislative assembly under the Directory, with great political talent and rare eloquence; it was then he had attempted to end the Revolutionary Wars which were bleeding the country dry. He also made no secret of favouring peace and the restoration of the monarchy.

'It was Bonaparte who stopped us by sending one of his henchmen, General Augereau, from Italy to round up the deputies in the assembly and shoot a few hundred royalists.' Pichegru shrugged. 'But then he did the same himself when he slaughtered the revolutionaries and national guardsmen who wanted to overthrow his friend Barras, and his directorate, in 1795.'

A patient listener, Réal let the general recount the sequel which he already knew. How Bonaparte had discovered evidence implicating Pichegru in the royalist conspiracy and alerted the Directory. Three months before, on the Rhine front, Moreau's cavalry had captured General de Kinglin, a Frenchman in Austrian service; his papers confirmed the contacts between Pichegru and the Prince of Condé to ensure the return of the Bourbons.

'But you must know about Kinglin,' Pichegru went on. 'Didn't they give you all his papers to examine?' Réal nodded. 'And you didn't discover anything about your master, Bonaparte?'

'No,' Réal said. 'Was there anything?'

'There might be. Kinglin knew the story.'

'What story?'

But Pichegru shut his mouth; he spun out the discussion as though loath to lose Réal's company, or perhaps unwilling to give Bonaparte and his lackeys a pretext for murdering him. Subtle and smooth as always, Réal let the subject drop for several days before suddenly announcing he had searched the Kinglin papers and found nothing about Bonaparte.

'It merely means they've destroyed the evidence,' Pichegru said.

'What evidence?'

Pichegru hesitated, then said, 'Evidence that Bonaparte was intriguing with Louis XVIII for the return of the Bourbons in the middle of his first Italian Campaign.'

'Do you have proof of this?' Réal asked, concealing his astonishment.

Pichegru nodded. 'He doesn't know this, but he only got half the secret papers when he captured the Comte d'Entraigues in Venice. The other half went to London.'

Out of a curious loyalty to the imprisoned general, and fear that such an accusation might endanger him, Réal said nothing to

Bonaparte about this interview. However, he could imagine the sensation Pichegru would create at the trial by pointing the finger at the First Consul and charging him with royalist intrigues. Such revelations might even spark off another revolution, inspired by diehard republicans.

Réal might have kept quiet altogether, except that Pichegru had another even more damning piece of testimony which he promised to disclose only to his judges. They were discussing the Pharaohs and their civilization when Pichegru gave a wry grin and said, 'How do you think Bonaparte got back from Egypt?'

'But everybody knows his frigate *Muiron* ran the blockade of the English fleet.'

'So, you imagine they slipped past Nelson, the most remarkable and dedicated of all English admirals. And this after he had annihilated our fleet at Aboukir[1] and was blockading the coast to prevent Bonaparte's army from leaving.'

'Isn't that the way of it?'

Pichegru shook his head.

'Then what is the explanation?' Réal insisted.

For several minutes, Pichegru fell silent as

---

[1] Battle of the Nile.

though weighing the consequences of replying, then he said, 'Let's say Nelson turned his blind eye on that frigate.'

'Why would he do that?'

'On his government's orders.'

'But why?'

'Because Bonaparte had secretly agreed with English diplomats that when he had overthrown the Directory, France would make peace with England and leave Europe alone.'

Réal grinned. 'That's a wild notion,' he said.

'That's not what they say in the highest circles in London.'

'Nobody can prove it.'

'Don't be too sure of that. Anyway, it makes sense. And with the evidence in the Entraigues papers proving complicity with the royalists, the public might judge for itself.'

Now Réal faced a dilemma and he had to make a choice. Pichegru or Bonaparte? His weeks with Pichegru had convinced him this honest and fearless general would carry out his threat to expose Bonaparte. With some trepidation, Réal did what he considered his duty and informed the First Consul of the insinuations made against him. 'Absurd,' Bonaparte snapped, dismissing them with a backhanded gesture. However, Réal noticed his wintry stare and that twitching shoulder. Pichegru's accusations had struck home.

'So, General Pichegru wants to turn the trial into a scandal and a farce with that rubbish dreamed up by Bourbon and English agents,' Bonaparte grunted. He paced up and down for several minutes then turned and snapped at Réal, 'Then let him — but first persuade him to tell you what else he's going to say to his judges.'

No matter how cunningly Réal chitchatted and quizzed, he learned nothing more. But around Pichegru, the atmosphere had altered. During Réal's visits he now observed several curious changes in prison routine. It seemed no one was any longer concerned that the general might take his own life, for both gaolers who had kept surveillance night and day in the cell had suddenly disappeared. From the prison concierge, Réal learned the general himself had objected to their permanent presence. And strangely, General Moncey, inspector-general of prisons, had implied that a powerful man like Pichegru might attack and injure his guardians. To Réal, all this rang false and he confided his fears to Bonaparte that Pichegru might be tempted to take his life if he found the means.

'I instructed them myself to leave General

Pichegru in peace,' the First Consul muttered. He gave Réal a hard look. 'Anyway, nobody can prevent a man from destroying himself.'

No, but one can make it easier for him, Réal reflected as he left the study. On the way downstairs, he heard spurs and a sword clanking and a figure he detested even more than Fouché and Talleyrand climbed past him without a glance. General René Savary, the brute who would stoop to any crime to please his master and ensure his own promotion. From the foot of the stairs he heard Savary's boot heels smack together in Bonaparte's antechamber. He would have given much to be a fly on a wall there.

Bonaparte led Savary into his empty study to discuss several dispositions of the gendarmerie before broaching the question of the prisoners and their trial. 'You know,' he murmured in Savary's ear, 'they say General Pichegru is growing desperate enough to kill himself.'

'He's afraid of the guillotine,' Savary said.

'That's it,' Bonaparte agreed. 'He cannot imagine himself going to the guillotine and he's sure I won't spare his life.' As an additional mark of esteem for Savary, he put a hand on his shoulder then said, 'Of course, it would be better for all of us if Pichegru didn't come to trial.'

Savary gazed at him for a full minute before grasping the import of that statement. He nodded slowly, saluted, then hurried downstairs like a man with an important mission.

13

A week later, on 7 April, one of Réal's inspectors came to his house to wake him with the news that General Pichegru had killed himself in his cell early that morning or late the previous night.

'Pichegru dead!' Réal gasped, sitting up in bed. 'But we made sure he had no means of committing suicide.'

'They say he strangled himself.'

A face and a name immediately flashed into Réal's mind: Savary. He recalled the urgent summons to Savary that day at the Tuileries just after Bonaparte and he had discussed Pichegru. Dressing hurriedly, he drove to the Temple Prison and mounted to the tower.

Already four magistrates had gathered in the cell, and as many doctors were discussing the autopsy. Réal looked at Pichegru's body, lying as they had found it on the rough wooden bed; his legs were spread-eagled and his left hand lay lax on the flagstoned floor; his head lolled; his tongue had extruded from his gaping mouth, and around his neck, biting into the livid flesh, was a black silk cravat through which a bit of wood a foot long had been thrust.

'Yes, that's how he died; he garrotted himself with that piece of wood, using it as a tourniquet to tighten the cravat,' one of the doctors said in answer to his query.

'But . . . but is that possible?' Réal said. 'Surely a man would release his grasp as he lost consciousness.'

'It is possible,' the doctor replied. 'There are cases — rare, certainly — in the medical literature.'

Réal picked up the Latin copy of Seneca's *Letters* from Pichegru's table, his mind going back to the discussion he and the general had had about the Roman philosopher. Someone had turned the page down at Cato's adieu before he killed himself rather than submit to Caesar —

Let the whole universe assemble under Caesar's banners, let his legions and ships take over the earth and the sea, Cato will still escape him and assure himself of a way to remain free.

Somehow, this piece of evidence struck a false note with Réal, who could not imagine a man like General Charles Pichegru leaving this as his dying testimony, or renouncing life without putting up a fight.

He took statements from the turnkey, the prison concierge and others who had seen or heard Pichegru the previous evening. It seemed the general had eaten his supper alone in his cell. After finishing ample helpings of soup, vegetables, stew and cheese and washing these down with red wine, he had ordered Sebastien Popon, the turnkey, to bring him a cup of brandy. Popon thought the general in good heart; his confessor, the Abbé de Keravenant, had given him communion the previous day and Desmarais, the police inspector, had procured him Seneca's *Letters* in Latin. At ten o'clock, the general was drowsing on his bed when Popon locked first the stout door, then the gate of the antechamber where a guard sat on duty. Not a sound came from the adjoining cells where Bouvet and Cadoudal lay; in the nearby wing, Chouan prisoners had received orders to keep quiet and stay away from their peepholes.

Popon watched Fauconnier, the concierge, playing cards with some of the minor prisoners. Just beyond midnight, they heard a grunting and coughing and sounds of a scuffle from the tower. Fauconnier rose and hurried to the top-security cells. Ten minutes later, he returned, muttering it was nothing.

But when he picked up his cards, his hands trembled so violently he could hardly hold them.

Next morning, Popon went to light a fire in the cell. Seeing the general asleep, he waited half an hour, but returned to find him still sleeping, which he had never done before. Approaching to wake him, he noticed Pichegru's face looked black and livid and seemed covered with bruises; a black cravat was twisted tight with a stick which was wedged under the angle of the jaw.

By the time Réal arrived at the Tuileries to report to Bonaparte, Savary had already given him all the details.

'A fine end for the Conqueror of Holland,' Bonaparte murmured to Réal. 'As for us, we've lost our best piece of evidence against Moreau.'

Réal knew his master and his machinations too well to take these remarks at their face value. As he descended the palace steps, he wondered why the man felt no guilt about Enghien and now about Pichegru when he himself was nearly crying for both those deaths, one a judicial assassination, the other a brutal murder, in his view.

Six doctors did the post-mortem and adduced evidence to show General Charles Pichegru had managed to garrotte himself in this unusual way; four obedient magistrates declared no inquiry was necessary; a government commissar announced Pichegru had proved his moral as well as material guilt by taking his own life.

They drove the Saviour of the Country through Paris, his simple hearse followed by one anonymous soldier; they shovelled him under the earth in an unnamed grave beside the body of another failed conspirator — Saint-Réjant.

In a corner of the Tuileries, Talleyrand glided over to Claire de Rémusat to murmur, softly, 'General Pichegru — now there's a man who died at the right time.'

14

As a piece of strategy and tactics, Bonaparte compared his march to the throne with the best of his military campaigns. Posterity, he felt, could hardly reproach him for striking back at the Duc d'Enghien as one of the family that had hired men to come and assassinate him, the elected ruler of France. Nor could it blame him for Pichegru's mysterious end, even if he overheard insistent whispers that Savart, the gaoler, had done the general to death on the orders of Bonaparte's lackey, General Savary.

Let them snigger. As long as they did not cry their suspicions aloud in the streets or back them with guns. He had exposed the treachery of royal princes and a renegade general and dealt with them ruthlessly enough to convince both monarchists and revolutionaries that only one man mattered in France: Bonaparte.

He had drawn Moreau's teeth and hoped his trial would finish him as a rival. He had manipulated the conspiracy to scare the army and the public, to show them how near they had come to losing him. What did two dead bodies and a handful of guillotined conspirators mean if they paved the way for an emperor? Those who had intended to murder him and usurp his power could now savour the supreme irony of having helped place a crown on his head.

He had judged the moment well. From the public and the assembly came pleas for him to assume plenary power — pleas cleverly inspired and fanned by Talleyrand and others. On 30 April, little more than three weeks after Pichegru's enigmatic death and a month after Enghien's murder, the Tribunate, primed and persuaded by Bonapartist deputies, voted to confer on Napoleon Bonaparte the title of Emperor of the French.

Only Lazare Carnot, one of the original revolutionaries, opposed the move, declaring Bonaparte a dictator and attacking the concept of hereditary monarchy. But once the motion was ratified by the legislative body, Bonaparte became emperor with the title descending to his male heirs, or to sons and grandsons of his brothers. Joseph and Louis were named as his heirs and the members of his family princes of the blood. Seventeen of his generals, including Murat, Bernadotte, Lannes, stepped up to become Marshals of France.

In the middle of May the entire senate

arrived to pay homage to the new emperor at Saint-Cloud. Dressed in a simple colonel's uniform, he received them like a king; by his side, his empress, Joséphine, was smiling, though people who knew her discerned tears behind the smile.

'Don't make yourself a king, Bonaparte,' she had pleaded, fearing he was flying too high. Or he would decide to sacrifice her as well to marry some young princess who would bear him heirs for his new dynasty.

In the great audience hall, Bonaparte replied to the eulogy spoken by Cambacérès. 'I accept the title which you have deemed beneficial for the glory of the nation. I submit to the people's sanction the law of heredity. I hope that France will never regret the honour which she confers on my family.'

Every crowned head of Europe sent his congratulations — except those of Russia, Sweden and England. It reminded him that his army was still camped on the cliffs around Boulogne. But for the threat to his personal security and his rule from the Cadoudal Conspiracy, his own involvement in foiling the plot and twisting it to his advantage, he would have invaded England and destroyed his most tenacious enemy. To boost its spirit, he and Joséphine visited the army on the Channel. There, his new marshals and men greeted the emperor and empress with elation, vowing to die for him, and France.

Yet, on his return, Paris appeared nervous. Bonaparte had always prided himself on walking the streets of his capital without fear of the assassin or public molestation, but now, he did not even venture out, as he had sometimes done in the past, disguised in bourgeois or even tradesmen's clothing. A truculent unrest seemed to hang over the city like a bad odour after the murder of Enghien and Pichegru's death. Those deeds had roused many voices against him and his postbag filled with anonymous threats, and unnamed writers peppered him with calumny in dozens of pamphlets.

On the Tuileries walls, he read slogans vilifying him and his rule. Royalists and Moreau's republican supporters joined together to menace his life. *Scoundrel! Do you think your crimes will go unpunished? Condemn Moreau to death and you will not survive him for two hours.* And on the Louvre, another saying, *Bonaparte, vile murderer, we're arming against you. You have just murdered Pichegru and the Duc d'Enghien, both innocent and unfortunate victims of your blood lust. Away with you, Monster.* Even in the barracks, he knew a signal had gone down the ranks, saying: *Soldiers, you have served under Moreau, you will be cowards if you let him die on the scaffold.*

Nevertheless, Paris went on a spree to celebrate imperial rule. Bonaparte's followers laid on parades, firework displays, circuses, exhibitions, concerts and dancing in the streets. Sounds of the singing and carousing carried over the thick façade of the Temple Prison to the tower where Cadoudal lay. Already, he had learned the representative bodies had voted to make the First Consul an emperor and the people would no doubt confirm this.

To Hozier who was allowed to see him for several minutes, he shrugged his massive shoulders and grunted, 'It seems I came to make a king and created an emperor.'

In ten days, on 28 May, their trial would begin.

15

Several days before the trial, Cadoudal saw Thuriot enter his cell with a tall man who limped from a thigh wound. For a moment, the Chouan wondered if his eyes were tricking him, then beneath the torn and dishevelled naval uniform, he recognized the figure of John Wright who had landed them at Biville and had fought so bravely over the years with the men of Brittany and La Vendée.

'Do you know this man?' Thuriot asked Wright, pointing at Cadoudal.

'I have never seen him in my life before,' Wright replied.

'And I don't suppose you can tell me who this British naval officer is?' Thuriot said, sarcastically, to Cadoudal.

'Your negative supposition is correct,' Cadoudal said.

Thuriot had them taken to the window overlooking the exercise yard. There, men from Wright's ship were laughing and joking with the Chouan prisoners. 'They know each other and make no secret of it,' Thuriot sneered. 'You might as well confess Monsieur

Wright landed you and your men on the French coast at Biville.'

When both men disclaimed this, the magistrate threatened the British officer with a court-martial and a firing squad, to which Wright replied, 'Do what you like, but I shall never betray my king, my country and my own honour.'

Wright knew the Temple having spent two years there after being taken prisoner with his uncle Sir Sidney Smith, with whom he escaped. He had fought beside Smith to halt Bonaparte at Saint-Jean d'Acre and had, in fact, saved Savary's life by rescuing him from the Turks.

But now, when Savary came to see him, it was to complain the British were flouting the rules of war by using assassins like the Chouans to commit murder for them. He promised Wright fair treatment if he made a full confession, but, realizing he could expect nothing from Savary, the naval captain refused to say anything. Nevertheless, Thuriot added to the list of charges against Cadoudal: intelligence with the enemy.

For his truculence, Savary forbade the wounded Wright every privilege, including the exercise hour, which even Cadoudal enjoyed. However, Wright persuaded a kindly prison doctor he must have some air.

Hobbling across the prison yard using a piece of wood as a crutch, he joined Cadoudal in a corner, surrounded by his men. 'I'm sorry we should meet here, Georges,' he whispered.

'We are where God has willed us,' Cadoudal replied, humbly. 'I was vain enough to believe God had placed a dagger in my hand to kill.'

'We're not finished yet.'

'No, John, but we've failed,' Cadoudal whispered. 'We've failed ourselves, we've failed the princes and we've failed France.'

Wright shook his head. 'That's not what they are saying in London.'

'Who are saying?'

'Your good friend Windham, and Pitt and others. They say the princes let you down because they had neither the heart nor the thought to join you.'

'Artois is an honourable man.'

Wright shrugged and fell silent for several minutes while the Chouans distracted the prison guards. 'You know no one in England can or ever will admit any association with you or your men — but if they could, they'd raise a monument to you.'

'A monument? I don't understand.'

'Bonaparte was on the point of invading and probably conquering England when you forced him to turn his full attention to the dangers he faced here, at home.'

'The little man merely used me to make himself emperor,' Cadoudal said, bitterly.

'No, he was worried about the conspiracy and the *coup d'état* — we know this. Especially the idea Moreau had thrown his lot in with you. So, you did as much as the Royal Navy to stop Bonaparte from leading his army across the Channel when he could well have succeeded.'

'Then I served some purpose.'

'More than you or most people will ever know.' Supporting his lame leg on the makeshift crutch, he seized Cadoudal's right hand and squeezed it with both of his. 'I shall pray for you, Georges,' he whispered. Then he turned away and limped back to his cell.

A week before the trial, the forty-seven prisoners had read to them the act accusing them of conspiracy against the state, of attempting to murder the First Consul and overthrow the lawful Government of France.

When the judges had gone, Cadoudal united his men and explained that in a week's time they would face trial. If anyone felt his courage faltering they should look to him, their general, knowing that he would suffer the same fate. He offered up a prayer, but he also gave them advice. Those who had revealed anything during interrogation must

276

retract such confessions before the court. Especially Bouvet de Lozier who must deny everything he had said to compromise General Moreau who might one day help the Bourbons to regain their rightful place. Above all, everyone must remain dignified and resolute.

Cadoudal realized Bonaparte had flouted the constitution and the law in decreeing a public trial to give the conspiracy and attempts to murder him the widest audience. Bonaparte knew no military tribunal would pass the death sentence on General Moreau, idol of the army. As president of the court, the First Consul had chosen Pierre-Charles Hémard, a hardened republican who had shown no mercy in judging Saint-Réjant and Carbon as well as Arena and Cerrachi for the two previous attempts to kill Bonaparte. To give Hémard free rein, a decree had abolished juries in cases of treason, assassination and other crimes against state security. Among the other nine magistrates figured Thuriot, notorious for his hatred of the Chouans.

Bonaparte took no chances. On the night of 27 May, he moved a whole division into place round the Temple and the Tuileries, sealing off all the routes leading to the Conciergerie, that grim prison on the Île de la Cité from which so many aristocrats and revolutionaries went to the guillotine during the Reign of Terror. Through this screen of thousands of soldiers moved three convoys of carriages taking the prisoners for the trial the next day.

16

When they filed into the huge judgment hall which had witnessed the most famous trials of the Revolution and its blood-letting, the prisoners could see that Parisian society had packed the public gallery, at least that part which gendarmes and detectives had left vacant.

Everyone was aware that Madame Jeanne Récamier, a bit older and perhaps not so beautiful as her famous portrait by Jacques-Louis David, had come to lend her friend, General Moreau, her moral support. Two tiers of aristocrats applauded the Polignac princes and the Marquis de Rivière. But most of the crowd had come to see General Georges Cadoudal, the Chouan leader who had vowed to kill Bonaparte and stage a *coup d'état.*

They found him nothing like his Press caricatures, for he had dressed elegantly in satin breeches and stockings, buckled shoes, ruffed shirt and black cravat under a dark-brown morning coat. He sat in dignified silence, his powerful features calm as he surveyed the panel of judges sitting with their

279

backs to the three immense windows of the old parliament chamber.

In black costume and cape, without decorations, Moreau occupied the front of the three benches filled by the forty-seven accused men. Cadoudal sat behind him.

For hours they listened as a clerk intoned the indictments, covering everything from the Chouan Wars to the infernal machine of Saint-Nicaise. All this time, Cadoudal had his head buried in a newspaper to show his contempt and indifference. Even when Hémard, the president, began to cross-question him, he kept on reading until Hémard lost his temper and shouted at him to put down the paper.

'Why did you come to France?'

'To see if there was a means of restoring the monarchy.'

'Who gave you the money they found on you?'

'I had it.'

'Where did it come from?'

'From funds I had to maintain my army when I was making war.'

'Where did you disembark?'

'You know.'

'I'm asking you.'

'I don't know the name of the place.'

'Who were you with?'

'I don't know them.'

'Where did you stay in Paris?'

'Nowhere.'

'Didn't you stay at Chaillot?'

'No.'

'When arrested didn't you lodge with a grocer?'

'When arrested I was in a cab and was staying nowhere.'

'Where did you sleep the night before you were arrested?'

'The night before I was arrested I didn't sleep.'

This antiphonal exchange mesmerized the crowd and from the strident tone and rising pitch of Hémard's voice contrasting with the calm and defiant responses of Cadoudal, they had no doubt who was winning the battle of wills. Cadoudal had done what he intended — set the pattern of their defence and given his men a lead. He refused to co-operate or put a name to anyone or anything, though obviously taking upon himself full responsibility for his actions.

'When did you start to serve in the royalist army?'

'In 1795.'

'How long did you serve?'

'Up to the moment of my arrest.'

After denying any part in the explosion of

Christmas Eve 1800, Cadoudal sat back to listen impassively as scores of witnesses followed one another through the long, torrid days of the trial. Only when his orderly, Louis Picot, came to testify did he show signs of emotion.

'Why did you come to Paris?'

In halting French, accented with his native Breton tongue, Picot said, 'I was attached to my master so I followed him.'

'You said you wanted to die for your king and country.'

'I might have said so. It would be my duty.'

Holding out his crushed fingers, he denied having said the Duc de Berri would land to join the Chouans; they had wrung this statement out of him in prison by scorching his feet and trapping his fingers in a vice. Cadoudal ended Picot's misery by declaring he knew nothing about the plot or even why they were in Paris.

Day after day, the trial continued with the flimsy evidence against the conspirators sounding more and more monotonous as each witness repeated it. But the mention of England's part in the plot and the appearance of Captain John Wright in the great hall enlivened the atmosphere. Accused by several witnesses of having plotted with the leaders of the British cabinet, Cadoudal denied this and the president shouted at him, 'Where are the proofs of this denial?'

'In the conscience of Monsieur Fouché,' Cadoudal replied.

John Wright had waited six days for his summons to the witness stand; he refused to walk on his wounded leg and they bore him, protesting, into the court and sat him in a chair.

'Do you promise to speak without hate and without fear?' Hémard asked.

Wright levered himself up. 'I am a prisoner of war. My name is John Wesley Wright. I claim the rights and usages of war — '

'That doesn't prevent you from saying what you know.'

'I am English and I know my duty to my king and country. I owe no account of my military conduct to anyone besides my government. I shall not reply to any questions put to me.'

At this, the public gallery erupted in applause until Hémard threatened to clear it. With Wright he got no further. Although suffering agony from his wound, the British captain stood firm: against Troche, the only man who claimed to recognize him; against the Temple gaoler who affirmed he was an escaped prisoner under the Directory; against Thuriot to whom he pointed, saying, 'You have failed to put in your report the fact they threatened to shoot me if I didn't betray state secrets.'

'It is mentioned in the second interrogation.'

'It *was* mentioned, until you struck it out,' Wright countered. Cheers from the gallery followed him as they carried him out.

Everyone was waiting to hear General Moreau. Already, the procurator-general, André Gérard, had accused him of having lured Cadoudal and his Chouans, then Pichegru, to Paris, of having promised the Bourbon princes and the British Cabinet he would support a bid to overthrow the First Consul. No one inside or outside the judgment hall doubted that Bonaparte desired only one verdict on his great rival: death. Yet, the public and even the judges were beginning to have misgivings about Moreau's guilt. On Cadoudal's orders, Bouvet had withdrawn his testimony which damned Moreau. Still, the procurator-general demanded the death penalty.

On the eighth day, Moreau rose amid applause which continued until Hémard had several spectators arrested. With great dignity, Moreau retraced his career as a soldier who had won victories like Hohenlinden and had served republican governments loyally. He had then resumed his private life without wishing to involve himself with the army or politics. Had he wished to conspire, surely he would have sought a military role to make it possible.

He ended his speech by crying, 'I protest in the face of Heaven and before men that I am innocent. You know your duty. France will heed you, Europe will contemplate you and posterity awaits your verdict.'

As he sat down, feet drummed then thundered on the gallery floor, and even some gendarmes in the chamber joined in. Hémard glowered, impotent to stop this clandestine applause.

Cadoudal turned to the Marquis de Rivière. 'If I were Moreau, I'd sleep tonight in the Tuileries,' he whispered.

If it had lost ground with Moreau, the court won it back with Aimé Joyaux, Coster-Saint-Victor and others whom it accused of having taken part in the Saint-Réjant plot. But with Cadoudal's example to follow, not one of them flinched. Asked for his definition of liberty, Joyaux shouted back, '*La Liberté*. It is to be where Bonaparte is not.'

To drumming applause, the Marquis de Rivière accused the court and the interrogators of having falsified testimony through torture or verbal trickery. He praised Cadoudal and made no attempt to deny having known him as an army leader in Brittany. Hémard halted him by holding up a miniature and crying, 'Accused Rivière, do you recognize this portrait?'

'It is the portrait of Monseigneur le Comte d'Artois who had the kindness to give it to me.' Asking to look more closely at the exhibit, he placed it to his heart then his lips, gazing at the exasperated flush on the president's face.

For thirteen interminable days the trial ran. Towards the end, each accused man had the chance to speak in his defence. Cadoudal confined himself to a few words. He had returned to France, he said, believing public opinion had shifted in favour of the Bourbons, but knowing also the moves and machinations to make Bonaparte a hereditary monarch.

'My aim in landing on French soil was to examine the possibility of turning opinion in favour of the Bourbon family. If I had believed the public favourable to that family, I would have straight away sent for a French prince. On his arrival, I would have calculated the means of achieving the desired result. But mistaken in my hopes, I did not send for the French prince or gather together even six men. This is the truth and no one can deny it.'

When the speeches ended, the judges rose and retired to deliberate. As they waited for the verdict, the prisoners heard 10,000 people outside the court clamouring for Moreau's acquittal, and some of them baying for Bonaparte's head. Whispers reached them that the magistrates were wrangling over Moreau's guilt or innocence, and Savary was shuttling between the court and his master, Bonaparte, who was issuing directives from the Tuileries.

At four in the morning, fourteen hours after retiring, the magistrates filed back. They called for twenty-two of the prisoners, who realized this first summons meant acquittal and freedom. Among them went Caron, who had offered Cadoudal his last cache, Spain who had made it and so many others who had helped the conspirators.

Silence fell over the public gallery as another five accused marched before the judges: Jules de Polignac, Moreau, Louis le Ridant, Mademoiselle Hisay and a Chouan named Rolland. They heard their guilt pronounced, but with a sentence not exceeding two years. Moreau went pale, turned on his heel and without a word or a salute to the court, quit the building by a side

287

door. Hailing a cab from the rank, he ordered the amazed driver to take him back to the Temple Prison.

To the twenty remaining accused, Hémard pronounced death by guillotine. Cadoudal shrugged. Bouvet de Lozier, Hozier, Coster Saint-Victor and Joyaux showed no emotion. But gasps and cries of No came from the public gallery at the death sentence passed on the Marquis de Rivière, aide and confidant of Artois, and Armand de Polignac, one of his favourites. Two of Pichegru's aides, General Frederic Lajolais and the Swiss major, François Rusillion, were also condemned.

Of the twenty, Cadoudal and Rivière appeared the least concerned. As they left the courtroom under escort to make their way back to the Conciergerie, Cadoudal said to the marquis, 'We've finished now with earthly kings, now we have to prepare to meet the King of Heaven.'

17

Handing Bonaparte the final verdicts, Savary had never before seen him so angry and bitter. Marching up and down his study, hands clenched behind his back, face twitching with rage, he heaped abuse on Régnier, Réal, Hémard and the cowardly bunch of magistrates who were scared for their own lives. Breaking stride, he spat at Savary, 'They've given Moreau a shop-lifter's sentence.'

What did he really care about the others, the misguided and empty-headed royalists and the wild bunch of Chouans? His arch-enemy had got away not only with his head but his reputation. 'Oh, I wouldn't have let him go to the guillotine,' he grunted at Savary, who stood mute. 'But branded with the death sentence and then pardoned, his name would have meant nothing more for anyone in France.' He paraded the room, holding a dialogue with himself. 'That man, Moreau! What can I do with him? Keep him as a rallying cry for every rebel and rascal? No, let him sell up and get out of the country. What would I do with him in the Temple? I have more than enough prisoners.'

He was still seething later that morning when Murat arrived in his brand-new marshal's uniform to plead for the lives of the twenty condemned men. Bonaparte listened, stony-eyed, as Murat urged him to exercise clemency in his own interest. 'They'll say the emperor forgives those who conspired against the First Consul,' he said. Bonaparte chased him out of the room.

Everyone, it seemed, wanted him to pardon the conspirators. Joséphine came to implore him, tearfully, to save Armand de Polignac and Rivière, meaning to plead for the others later. Claire de Rémusat begged for several men until Bonaparte rounded to snap at her, 'So you, too, take the part of people who would assassinate me.'

He refused to listen. His spies brought word Joséphine was receiving the wives and relatives of condemned noblemen in her own apartments and this infuriated him even more. 'You seem only interested in people who think my life's too cheap to bother about,' he told her.

She and Claire de Rémusat watched the shuffling, gliding figure of Talleyrand enter Bonaparte's apartments. He gave them a slight bow and they knew that if he had played a devious part in the Enghien murder, he would not advocate more bloodshed which would merely antagonize the royalist faction. When he emerged, his wigged head twitched a fraction, indicating he had suceeded. This time, Bonaparte did not shut the door in his empress's face and muttered he would grant Madame de Polignac an audience.

Yet, he did not spare the feelings of Armand de Polignac's beautiful wife. 'You ask me for the life of a man who wished to take mine,' he said, then added with gallantry, 'But how can I say no to someone so heartrending in her misfortune?' Cutting short her thanks, he finished the interview by declaring, 'The really guilty ones are those who engage their friends in such mad and criminal enterprises. At the very least, they should share the perils of the young men whose lives they put in danger.' And with that warning to the Bourbon princes, he dismissed her.

Two small nephews came to beg for their uncle, Marquis Charles de Rivière and with Bonaparte's assurance went to the Conciergerie to inform him his life was spared. To save Bouvet de Lozier, Caroline Bonaparte acted as intermediary. As for Charles d'Hozier, how could he guillotine the son of the man who had recognized the nobility of the Bonapartes and thus secured his entry to the Brienne military school? Lajolais and

Rusillion and Rochelle, friends and lieutenants of Pichegru also received the imperial grace as did Armand Gaillard, the only Chouan.

But Bonaparte turned a deaf ear to suggestions of a pardon for Coster-Saint-Victor; he knew his royalist clique of friends would snigger that poor Coster was losing his head out of imperial jealousy because he had slept with Mlle George. But Bonaparte had no recollection of ever having seen the most dandified of the Chouans in Avenue de Provence. No, Coster and Joyaux would pay the supreme debt because they had twice tried to kill him, once with Saint-Réjant and now with Cadoudal.

And Georges Cadoudal? He had not asked for mercy. And no one had even come to intercede for him or to shed tears over him. He had a sweetheart, that sister of his dead friend, Mercier. Why didn't she come to plead for him? No Corsican, brought up in the clan system would have failed a loved-one or a friend like that, he reflected. Even that gypsy, Murat, had come to ask for magnanimity and mercy for Cadoudal and the others. His old secretary and classmate, Bourrienne, had amplified the appeal.

'Look here, Bourrienne,' Bonaparte said, 'I have a certain regret about Cadoudal. He's a man of steel and he'd have done great things with me. But he wouldn't even listen to Réal when he proposed to give him a command under me. What can I do? He's too dangerous to let live.'

'Do you have to make conditions, sire?'

'If I don't make an example of some of them, England will cast all the riff-raff of the emigration on our shores.' He paused, then muttered, 'But Cadoudal is worth two of Moreau.'

*   *   *

For a week the condemned men waited in the Conciergerie. They had the privilege of ordering their meals from a restaurant in the Île Saint-Louis and neither Cadoudal nor the other leaders lacked the money to buy their men the best food and wines. On 15 June, a court usher entered and solemnly read a list of eight names: Polignac, Rivière, Bouvet, Hozier, Lajolais, Rochelle, Armand Gaillard and Rusillion. 'These prisoners will return to the Temple,' he said.

When the eight men had gathered their belongings together and were waiting for the prison wagon, Cadoudal took Charles d'Hozier aside. 'My old friend, maybe you'll see Louis XVIII on the throne. Tell him the best thing

293

he can do in my memory is recognize the services of my faithful comrades.'

Hardly had they left than the twelve remaining men were trundling south in a prison van to the most sinister of all French prisons — Bicêtre. Peopled first by the senile, then the insane and criminal, it had become the last halt before the guillotine.

There, in the early hours of 16 June, the twelve men exchanged their clothing for the convict's striped smock and trousers and deposited 1600 francs to feed them during their ten-day stay. They traversed a bleak courtyard lit by flaring lanterns where Dr Joseph-Ignace Guillotin had carried out the first experiments with dead bodies on the execution machine bearing his name.

At Bicêtre, they were installed in the white dungeons, ironically named because they caught lamplight from the long corridors when the peepholes opened occasionally. Cadoudal looked at the grim hole, its walls dripping, its plaster indented and scratched with names and dates, sole record and epitaph of so many unknown criminals and martyrs.

His men must feel as he did, downcast and demoralized at the sight of this black antechamber to eternity. He put his mouth to the peephole and bellowed, 'Let us pray, men.' And they prayed for the king, their fallen comrades and for their own souls, twelve voices echoing along the corridor.

When they met in the exercise yard for an hour in the morning and afternoon, he kept up their spirits by saying eight men had already been pardoned and other pardons must surely follow. He himself had written to Murat, asking for Bonaparte's mercy for his men. When Murat pointed out he had omitted his own name from the list, he grunted that it had taken enough heart-searching to beg favours for others: he had no intention of pleading with Bonaparte for his own life.

Several times they tried to persuade him to change his mind. First, Réal had whispered the emperor might look favourably on his written demand for grace; then the Marquis de Lauriston, Bonaparte's most handsome general and great-nephew of John Law, the Scot who had founded the French national bank, came to beseech Cadoudal to make the request. To both men he said, no.

As a final effort, Réal brought a letter he himself had written to Bonaparte to win a pardon. Cadoudal read only the first line — 'To His Majesty, Emperor of the French' — then handed it back to the state councillor, thanking him for his trouble.

'But why go to the guillotine when all you have to do is sign this?' Réal gasped.

'Can you promise me a better occasion to die?' Cadoudal replied.

Réal shook the Chouan general's massive hand and said goodbye for the last time. When he had gone, Cadoudal went down on his knees in the mud of his dungeon and prayed. He had as much dread of dying as most men and he asked God, who had given him the will and courage to fight well and live well now to allow him to die well.

He might have signed Réal's letter; he could have retired as a wealthy and honoured man to his native Brittany; he could also have renounced his vow never to marry until a Bourbon ruled France; he and Lucrèce could have lived out their lives in peace. Yet, it would have meant deserting these eleven men he had led into this adventure; it would have meant forsaking everything he held dear. Had he signed that letter he could never have lived with himself.

He preferred to suffer his calvary and die.

18

Just after midnight, a gendarme captain entered Cadoudal's dungeon and made an inventory of the few belongings that remained to him — his well-thumbed, leather-bound Bible which had accompanied him everywhere for ten years, a towel, several handkerchiefs, stockings and shoes. When he had finished, the captain searched him. His lantern light glittered on something around Cadoudal's thick neck and he held out his hand.

For a moment, Cadoudal hesitated before removing the thin gold chain with its cross and its ivory miniature framed in gold filigree. For a second, the gendarme glanced at the two portraits, on one side the jowly face of Louis XVI, on the other the delicate and fragile contours of a beautiful woman. Cadoudal observed him wrap it with the other articles as though it meant nothing. 'We leave in ten minutes,' the captain grunted, as he closed and locked the door.

So today he would come face to face with Henri Sanson, his executioner, submit to the scarlet embrace of Madame Guillotine. And, he trusted, meet his Maker. Well, a man had to die sometime, it was merely a question of when. And how. A million eyes would follow every gesture, every expression. He must not falter, but say what he had to say on behalf of his God and his king and die bravely.

When he knelt, he did not pray for himself but for Lucrèce, asking God to give her courage to confront life when he had gone. Now, their flesh and blood would never be united, yet they would wed in spirit for all eternity beyond this day of his death and hers. For Lucrèce, sister of his blood-brother, Pierre Mercier, would keep the faith.

More than he could say for the Bourbon princes who had promised everything and done nothing. Now he realized neither Artois nor Berri had ever set foot outside London, let alone embarked for France.

Pitt, the Englishman, had read their characters well when he had asked a year ago whether he could depend on the princes. Would they even suffer a moment of contrition for their general and his eleven officers and men whose heads Sanson would parade in front of the multitude this morning? Would it even deflect their minds from more important matters like their minuets and gavottes and endless card games? Yet, he had no rancour, only pity for their lack of resolution.

Twelve doors suddenly banged open and they assembled in the corridor lit by guttering lamps, all of them blinking like night birds. Both wrists and ankles manacled, they shuffled to the huge wagon with its separate cells. Once locked inside, they lumbered through the sleeping suburbs of Paris and clattered over cobbled streets on the one-hour journey to the Conciergerie. On arriving, Cadoudal threw himself on the bed in his cell, shut his eyes and fell asleep.

When he woke, dawn was filtering through the barred windows and a guard told him it was half-past five. Coster-Saint-Victor was grumbling they might have given him a decent costume to die in. 'I look like some circus clown in this,' he said, pointing to his convict's uniform. Louis Picot sat numb, lamenting having to die at 28 while Aimé Joyaux and Michel Roger were chatting nonchalantly.

At seven o'clock, the twelve men gathered in the same room for their final meal of cold meats, bread, wine and brandy. While they ate, a magistrate came to announce that the eight men convicted with them and sentenced to death had all received the emperor's grace. With Cadoudal, the others raised their glasses to toast those lucky enough to have escaped the guillotine.

Now they could hear the hubbub as the crowd thickened along the route from the Conciergerie to the Place de Grève where the scaffold stood. Those who had something to bequeath made their wills or communicated their last intentions verbally to Citizen Vel, the prison concierge. Cadoudal merely stated he wished to pay his lawyer 580 francs; he left nothing to anyone else, considering such bequests would only embarrass and perhaps incriminate them.

Twelve priests flitted silently into the room to hear the condemned men's confessions, the murmured dialogue losing itself in the insistent hum that penetrated the room from the crowd outside.

At ten o'clock, three more men dressed in sober clothing entered. No one needed telling that the tallest with the bleakest face was Henri Sanson, son of Charles Sanson, executioner of Louis XVI. Already, the son had 3,000 heads to his count. Curious, Cadoudal thought, he had always pictured Sanson in black tights with a black hood over his head and not like some bourgeois in silk top-hat, silk cravat, morning coat and brown buckskin breeches.

Sanson and his lieutenants, Desmarais and Legros got busy cutting the prisoners' hair to bare the nape of the neck; then the executioner had them unshackled and their hands bound behind their backs with rope. Like a drum roll, they caught the rattle of three tumbrils on the cobbled courtyard outside.

As they took their seats, Louis Picot gave a sob. 'Don't be an infant,' Cadoudal growled. No Chouan must show weakness.

Now the crowd had massed around them to such an extent the gendarmes had to beat a passage for the tumbrils; on observing the twelve men in the three carts, the people had gone strangely quiet. As far as the eye travelled, Cadoudal could see the *quais* on both sides of the Seine overflowing with men, women and even children who had come to enjoy the bloody spectacle on this burning June day. His eye took in the twin towers of Notre Dame, etched against the blue sky as they turned to cross the Pont au Change to the right bank of the river.

Their wagons seemed borne aloft on the crowd which pressed so closely around them it muffled the din of the wheels; along the Quai des Grèves, Savary's gendarmes had to flail at people with the flat of their sabres to clear a passage. Every minute seemed an age. Then, as they veered left, they saw her: our Lady Guillotine.

So often in those weeks when he lay in the

301

Temple waiting for his trial then after his condemnation, Cadoudal only had to shut his eyes to imprint on his mind the spectre of this macabre instrument. So familiar had it grown, he felt he had prepared himself for his final ordeal.

Yet a cold frisson ran from his neck to the base of his spine as he observed its black silhouette against the ornate façade of the town hall; its platform appeared to float on the rippling sea of faces, bicorn hats, shakos and plumed helmets of the infantry and cavalry surrounding it. Would his legs carry him up those five steps leading to the platform on which the swing board rested?

His gaze went to the semi-circular segments on the headpiece then up the tall frame, fully thirty feet high, to where the heavy, triangular blade scintillated in the June sun. Sanson and his two assistants were testing the pulley-ropes, egged on by the crowd which had wedged into the vast square, or clung to the windows of the town hall and other public buildings, or squatted on the parapets above the Seine.

Finally, the three tumbrils thrust their way to the foot of the scaffold and the twelve men descended with the three priests who accompanied them. Cadoudal stepped forward, his bulky figure dwarfing the shape of the executioner.

'I wish to go first,' he said.

'It is not the custom,' Sanson replied.

'Never mind the custom, I go first to set my men an example.'

After a moment, the headsman nodded.

A hush had fallen over the crowd. Cadoudal looked around him, then moved along the line of his men. With his hands bound behind his back he could only make the semblance of an embrace; first, he touched Louis Picot's wet cheek with his own, whispering that death was no more than a moment of pain; he said adieu to his loyal aide, Aimé Joyaux and others along the rank, ending with Coster-Saint-Victor, still smiling and holding his head erect.

'We shall meet in Heaven,' Cadoudal murmured.

They all watched him as he retraced his way, knowing he had another reason for offering his head first — he wanted to assure each of them he had not been secretly reprieved.

As he put his foot on the first of the steps, his confessor, the Abbé de Keravenant, held a cross over his head and recited the last Ave. 'Hail Mary, Mother of God, pray for us poor sinners now . . . Finish it,' he urged.

'What's the use of saying 'at the hour of our death',' Cadoudal replied 'I am there now?'

On the scaffold, he gazed at Sanson. 'Show my head to my comrades so that they know I shall not survive them,' he said.

He turned towards the crowd to proclaim for the last time allegiance to God and the king. But when he went to speak, a roll of drums set the still air vibrating and drowned his voice. Shrugging his huge shoulders, he stepped back and let Sanson and the two others strap him to the board which swung him into a horizontal position. They clamped the two wooden segments round his neck. As he heard Sanson make to release the pulley and let the heavy blade fall, Cadoudal summoned all his strength. His bull voice rose high above the beat of the drums:

'*Vive le Roi! Vive le Roi! Vive le —* '

Sanson brandished the severed head in front of the eleven men who waited their turn at the foot of the scaffold, then showed it to the crowd. The blue eyes had not yet lost their living sheen, and the open mouth appeared to frame the word *Roi* as though the guillotine had caught and petrified his final cry.

Such a silence gripped the crowd as Sanson threw the head into the basket after the body that the creak of the pulley ropes and the hiss of the blade in its grooves carried across the vast square as it ascended for the second man.

19

At 11.30 that morning, Bonaparte was pacing his study, dictating to Méneval. To the secretary, it seemed the emperor's shoulder twitch had suddenly grown worse, and he mumbled even more unintelligibly than usual.

Méneval's quill raced over the paper, but he still had to leave great gaps, first in the army order to the English invasion force at Boulogne, then in the instructions for the emperor's coronation later that year. To make things more trying, the racket of the throng around the Place de Grève drifted downriver and filtered through the high, arched windows of the study, which lay open on that hot day.

Suddenly, Bonaparte rounded and bawled, 'Constant, shut these windows . . . all of them, immediately.' His valet hastened to obey. But still a dull resonance filled the sunlit room.

Then, a loud drumbeat followed by a great roar set the windows vibrating and the air thrumming around the two men in the study. After that, absolute silence.

Bonaparte halted abruptly — both in his stride and speech. Méneval was certain that he quickly and surreptitiously made the sign of the cross. Then he stood for a long moment, his head bowed as though in prayer, or in silent homage to an enemy who had just died bravely, before resuming his dictation.

Epilogue

Ten years later, after Napoleon's exile to Saint Helena and during the Restoration, the bones of Georges Cadoudal were recovered. Baron Larrey, the Emperor's surgeon, had been using the magnificent skeleton to teach anatomy students at L'Hôtel-Dieu hospital in Paris. Consecrated, they now lie in a mausoleum constructed beside his birthplace at Kerléano in Brittany with those of his friend, Pierre Mercier, discovered in an attic at Loudeac in 1871. Lucrèce Mercier sought refuge with the Ursuline sisters at Château-Gontier; she took the veil when Cadoudal's remains had been consecrated, and Louis XVIII had returned to the throne. She died as Mother Superior in 1831. Napoleon had a strange, almost fateful revenge on Moreau. In 1813, at the Battle of Dresden where Moreau was advising the Russian Tsar how to beat Napoleon, a French cannonball shattered his legs and killed him. The Duc d'Enghien, still in the rags of his hunting clothes, was disinterred from his moat and reburied in hallowed ground; so, too, were the remains of General Charles Pichegru, which lie in his birthplace at Arbois in eastern France. Finally, the brave Captain John Wright never left the Temple Prison. A year after the Cadoudal trial he was found dead, his head almost severed by an open razor. A copy of the official *Le Moniteur* recounting the victory of Austerlitz and a map of the Danube area lay beside his body. Few people believed in his suicide. Those who studied the case point to the similarities with Pichegru's death — the props, the presence of the evil gaoler, Savart, and the sinister appearances at the prison of the no less evil General René Savary, later elevated to be Duc de Rovigo.

Bibliography

ON NAPOLEON BONAPARTE

Aubry, Octave *Vie Privé de Napoléon*, Flammarion Paris, 1939

Bainville, Jacques *Napoléon* Plon Paris, 1935

Las Cases, Comte de *Mémorial de Sainte Hélène* Garnier Frères Paris, 1895

Lockhart, J.G. *Life of Napoleon* Dent London, 1906

Madelin, Louis *Napoléon* Hachette Paris, 1958

Pautre, Léon *Entretiens avec Napoléon* Pierre Belfond Paris, 1969

Picard, Ernest *Bonaparte et Moreau* Plon Paris, 1905

Romains, Jules *Napoléon par Lui-Même* Perrin Paris, 1963

Vox, Maximilien *Napoléon* Seuil Paris, 1959

ON GEORGES CADOUDAL

Cadoudal, Georges de (Nephew) *Georges Cadoudal* Plon Paris, 1887

Castries, Duc René de *La Conspiration de Cadoudal* De Duca Paris, 1964

Chiappe, Jean-François *Georges Cadoudal ou La Liberté* Perrin Paris, 1971

Lenotre, G. *Georges Cadoudal* Grasset Paris, 1929

La Varende, Comte Jean de *Cadoudal* Editions d'Amsterdam Paris, 1952

Gassier, J.N. *Vie de Cadoudal* Aubry Paris, 1814

MISCELLANEOUS

Bourrienne, Louis Antoine Fauvelet de *Mémoires* Garnier Frères Paris, 1899

Daudet, Ernest *La Police et les Chouans* Plon Paris, 1912

Gassier, J.M. *Vie de Général Pichegru* Aubry Paris, 1814

Hauterive, Ernest de *La Contre-Police Royaliste en 1800*, II vols Perrin Paris, 1908–13

Lascelles, Edward *Life of Charles James Fox* OUP London, 1936

Mahan, Alfred Thayer *Life of Nelson*, II vols

Sampson Low London, 1897

Madelin, Louis *Fouché* Club des Editeurs Paris, 1960

Melchior-Bonnet, Bernardine *Duc d'Enghien Vie et Mort du Dernier des Condé* Amiot-Dumont Paris, 1955

Orieux, Jean *Talleyrand ou le Sphinx Incompris* Club Français Du Livre Paris, 1973

Pair, Georges *Messieurs Sanson, Bourreaux* Editions de France Paris, 1938

Rapp, Général Jean *Mémoires* Garnier Frères Paris, 1895

Regis, Roger *Joséphine* Librairie Chaussée-d'Antin Paris, 1944

Remacle, Comte *Relations Secrètes des Agents de Louis XVIII* Plon Paris, 1899

Rose, J. Holland *Life of William Pitt* II vols Bell London, 1912

Russell, Lord John *Life and Times of Charles James Fox* Bentley London, 1859–66

Saint-Hilaire, Emile Marco de *Histoire des Conspirations* Charles Felleus Paris, 1851

Saint-Ivy, G. de *La Chouannerie et ses Victimes* Auger Pontivy, 1909

Sommervogel, Gilbert *Correspondence du Duc de Berri* Perrin Paris, 1963

Stenger, Gilbert *La Société Française pendant le Consulat* Perrin Paris, 1903–8

Warner, Oliver *A Portrait of Lord Nelson*

Chatto and Windus London, 1958
Weiner, Margery *The French Exiles 1789–1815*
John Murray London, 1960–63
Welschinger, Henri *Le Duc d'Enghien*
Plon-Nourrit Paris, 1913
Wilson, Philip W. *William Pitt the Younger*
Doubleday, Doran New York, 1930
Zweig, Stefan *Fouché* Grasset Paris, 1931
Général de Caulaincourt, Baron de Méneval, Marquise de Rémusat, Comte Réal, Général Savary, Duc de Rovigo: *Memoires*

We do hope that you have enjoyed reading this large print book.

Did you know that all of our titles are available for purchase?

We publish a wide range of high quality large print books including:
Romances, Mysteries, Classics
General Fiction
Non Fiction and Westerns

Special interest titles available in large print are:
The Little Oxford Dictionary
Music Book
Song Book
Hymn Book
Service Book

Also available from us courtesy of Oxford University Press:
Young Readers' Dictionary
(large print edition)
Young Readers' Thesaurus
(large print edition)

For further information or a free brochure, please contact us at:
Ulverscroft Large Print Books Ltd.,
The Green, Bradgate Road, Anstey,
Leicester, LE7 7FU, England.
Tel: (00 44) 0116 236 4325
Fax: (00 44) 0116 234 0205

THE DAMNED

John D. MacDonald

A mixed group of American tourists never expected to be trapped together, unable to cross the river to continue their journey. They were all strangers and didn't really want to get to know each other, but the stalled river ferry takes away the luxury of choice. Under the brutal Mexican sun their personal relationships, their values and dreams are exposed in a way that leaves them no excuses. Their lives would never be the same again — and crossing that river was not even to be a journey they all would make . . .